Paul Leicester Ford

Some materials for a bibliography of the official publications

of the Continental Congress

1774-1789

Paul Leicester Ford

Some materials for a bibliography of the official publications of the Continental Congress
1774-1789

ISBN/EAN: 9783337233921

Printed in Europe, USA, Canada, Australia, Japan

Cover: Foto ©Raphael Reischuk / pixelio.de

More available books at **www.hansebooks.com**

BOSTON PUBLIC LIBRARY

Bibliographies of Special Subjects

ORIGINALLY PUBLISHED IN THE BULLETINS
OF THE LIBRARY

No. 6

SOME MATERIALS

FOR A

Bibliography of the Official Publications

OF THE

CONTINENTAL CONGRESS

1774-89

COLLECTED AND ANNOTATED BY

PAUL LEICESTER FORD

BOSTON
PRINTED BY ORDER OF THE TRUSTEES
1890

Some Materials for a Bibliography of the Official Publications of the Continental Congress.

1774-1789.

In 1885 the United States government published what purported to be *A Descriptive Catalogue of the Government Publications of the United States, September 5, 1774–March 4, 1881,* which should have rendered any such list as the present unnecessary; but that elaborate work was misnamed, as it is at best but an index to government publications, and for the period covered by this bibliography is little more than an imperfect index to the Journals of the Continental Congress, and has, therefore, been of no assistance in compiling this catalogue. From Sabin's *Dictionary of Books relating to America;* Thomas's and Haven's *Catalogue of Publications in the United States, 1639–1775,* and Hildeburn's *Issues of the Pennsylvania Press,* I have derived aid, more especially from the latter. I also owe thanks to Dr. Samuel A. Green, Hon. A. R. Spofford, Mr. F. A. Bancroft, Mr. Charles A. Cutter, Mr. W. Eames, Mr. Bumford Samuels, Mr. Lindsay Swift, Mr. William Kelby, and Mr. J. W. M. Lee, for assistance in the compilation.

The arrangement is strictly chronological, under the date of the Introduction by the committee, or the adoption by the Congress, and those without date and collected publications are placed at the end of the year to which they belong. The initials at the end of the description indicate certain public libraries in which the publication can be consulted.

A.	signifies	Astor Library.
A.A.S.	"	Am. Antiquarian Society Library.
B.	"	Boston Public Library.
B.A.	"	Boston Athenæum Library.
B.M.	"	British Museum Library.
C.	"	Library of Congress.
H.	"	Library of Harvard University.
M.	"	Massachusetts Historical Society Library.
My.H.S.	"	Maryland Historical Society Library.
N.J.H.S.	"	New Jersey Historical Society Library.
N.	"	New York Historical Society Library.
P.H.S.	"	Pennsylvania Historical Society Library.
P.	"	Library Company of Philadelphia.
P.L.	"	Private Library.
S.	"	New York State Library.
S.D.	"	Department of State Library.
...	"	A line omitted in the title.
.....	"	Two or more lines omitted in the title.
*	"	That what is omitted is line for line the same as the preceding title.
+	"	That what is omitted is already sufficiently given in title of previous edition.

PAUL LEICESTER FORD.

1774

Sept. 22. Preliminary non-importation resolve.

1. Philadelphia, / In Congress, Thursday, September 22, 1774. / Resolved, / ..... / [Philadelphia:] Printed by W. and T. Bradford.
4°. Broadside. P.

Oct. 20. Non-importation, &c. agreement.

2. The / Association, &c. [Philadelphia: Printed by W. and T. Bradford. 1774.]
8°. pp. 11. B.A., C., P.L.

An agreement between the twelve Colonies not to trade with England, drafted by Thomas Cushing, Isaac Low, Thomas Mifflin, Richard Henry Lee, and Thomas Johnson, Jun.

"Ordered, That this Association be committed to the press, and one hundred and twenty copies struck off." Journal as printed in *Force,* fourth series, 1.

The original document is reproduced in Force's *Archives,* fourth series, 1., 915; and a [burlesque] "versified and set to music" version was printed by Rivington in New York. There were also many pamphlets issued at the time, discussing it from all points of view.

3. The following Extract from the Votes and Pro-/ceedings of the American Continental Congress, / we are induced to publish thus early purely to / ease the Impatience of our Readers. / Association, &c. [New York:?] 8°.
pp. 8. N.

4. The following Extracts from the Votes and Proceedings of the American / Continental Congress, we are induced to publish thus early purely to ease / the Impatience of our Readers. / Association, &c. / ..... / Boston: Printed by Edes & Gill. F°. Broadside. M.

Oct. 21. Address and Memorial.

5. To the / People of Great-Britain, / from the / Delegates, / Appointed by the several English Co-/lonies ... / ...... / ... to consider of / their Grievances in General Con-/gress, at Phila-delphia, Septem-/ber 5th, 1774. / .. [Philadelphia : Printed by W. and T. Bradford. 1774.] 8°. pp. 36. P.L.

Two letters from the Congress, one to the "People of Great Britain" (drafted by John Jay), and the other to the "Inhabitants of the Colonies" (drafted by Richard Henry Lee), which were reported by a committee of three, — Richard Henry Lee, William Livingston, and John Jay. This title is not in Hildeburn, but, misled by Sabin (40,508), he gives a title of what is apparently the same pamphlet. Sabin was in error in the date, and the true description is given herein. No. 54.

"*Ordered*, That the Address to the people of *Great Britain*, and the Memorial to the Inhabitants of the *British* Colonies be immediately committed to the press; and that no more than one hundred and twenty copies of each be struck off, without further orders from the Congress." *Journal*.

The text of the letter to the "Inhabitants of the Colo-nies" was slightly altered in the subsequent issues, and copies of this edition are sometimes found with MS. cor-rections of the changes made.

5ª. To / Letters / from the / American Conti-nental Congress, / held / At Philadelphia, Sept. 5, 1774. / The one Addressed to the / People of Great Britain, / And the other to the / Inhabitants of the American Colonies. / Coventry : / Printed and Sold by J. W. Piercy, in Broad-gate. 1775. / (Price Two-pence.) 8°. pp. (4), 22. P.L.

6. A Letter to the People of Great Britain from the Delegates of the American Congress in Philadelphia. [London :] Andrews. 8°.

This title is taken from the "Monthly Catalogue" in the *Critical Review* from January, 1775 (xxxix, 73), where it is noticed as follows : —

". . . . It is a mixture of compliment and expostulation, accompanied with complaints relative to the establishment of the Catholic religion in Canada, and to the supposed violation of their privileges in the article of taxation; interspersed with ominous anticipations of the future slavery of the whole British dominion, in consequence of the plan of government adopted by administration. With respect to the Quebec Bill, it was only fulfilling engage-ments which we were solemnly bound to maintain by treaty of peace, and for the performance of which the national faith had been pledged. In regard to the point of taxation, we might have expected that the Americans would enter largely into the discussion of the subject, upon political principles; and that they likewise would have at least attempted to invalidate the force of the several precedents produced to evince their own acknowl-edgment or former acquiescence in the supreme authority of the British Parliament. Nothing of this kind is, how-ever, to be found in the Letter before us; a most material and unaccountable defect, if we consider that it was writ-ten at a time when the delegates, by whom it is sent, were upon the eve of adopting such extraordinary measures, as may endanger the whole system of British and American commerce."

Oct. 26. Letter to Quebec.

7. A Letter / to the / Inhabitants / of the / Province / of / Quebec. / Extract 'from the Minutes of the Congress. / Philadelphia : / Printed by William and Thomas Bradford, / October, 1774. / 8°. pp. (2), [37]-50. P.H.S.

Cushing, Lee and Dickinson were appointed, *October* 21, a committee to prepare this letter, the draft of which, both by common acceptance and by the statement in Dickinson's "*Writings*" (published in 1801, under his supervision), is referred to Dickinson's pen; yet John Adams (Diary in "*Works,*" 11., 392), on *October* 4, writes, "General Lee came to my lodgings, and showed me Address from the C. to the people of Canada, which he had " — or, eleven days before Dickinson was elected to the Congress, and eighteen days before the committee was appointed.

8. To the / Inhabitants / Of the Province of / Quebec. / From the / Continental Congress,

at Philadelphia, / September 5, 1774. / [Colo-phon.] Printed by John Holt, in Dock-Street. [New York : 1774.] 4°. pp. 7. P.L.

9. Ein Schreiben / An die / Einwohner / der / Pro-vinz / Quebec. / Auszug aus dem Protocoll des Con-gresses. / Philadelphia, / Gedruckt und zu haben bey Henrich Miller, /1774. / 8°. pp. (2), [63]-76.

10. Lettre / adressée / Aux Habitans / de la Province / de / Quebec, / Ci-devant le Canada. / De la part du Congrés Général de l'Am-/erique Septentrionale, tenu à Philadelphie. / Imprimé & publié par Ordre du Congrès. / A Phila-delphie, / De l'Imprimerie de Fleury Mesplet. / M.DCC.LXXIV. 8°. pp. (2), 18. P.

Translated by M. Du Simitiere, and two thousand copies printed for distribution in Canada.

11. A / Clear Idea / Of the General and Uncorrupted / British Constitution : / in an / Address to the Inhabitants / of the / Province of Quebec. / From the Forty-nine Delegates in the Continental / Congress at Philadelphia; / September 5, to October 10, 1774. / Extracted from the Votes and Proceedings. [London : Dilly and Almon, 1774.] 8°. pp. 8. M.

12. Extract, from the Journal of the proceed-ings, of the ho-/norable the American Continental Congress, ... / ... Being that part / of their Ad-dress to the Inhabitants of the Province of / Que-bec, which enumerates, the glorious rights of / Englishmen, ... / [Philadelphia : Printed by R. Bell, 1776.] 8°. pp. (6).

Usually found as a supplement to "Plain Truth..... By Candidus. Philadelphia, 1776."

Oct. 26. Petition to the King.

13. (133) / To Peyton Randolph, Esq. [Phila-delphia : W. and T. Bradford. 1774.] 8°. pp. [133]-144. P.L.

Printed as an appendix to No. 39, but copies were sepa-rately issued. It consists of the letter from Gage to Ran-dolph and the Petition to the King.

The Petition was reported to Congress by a committee consisting of John Adams, Thomas Johnson, Patrick Henry, John Rutledge, Richard Henry Lee, and John Dickinson, and the draft is claimed for both of the latter two : for Lee in his *Life* by R. H. Lee, Jr., and for Dickin-son in his *Writings*. The fair inference seems to be that Lee prepared the first draft, reported to Congress October 21, which, not meeting with their approval, was recom-mitted, with Dickinson added to the committee. The sec-ond report was probably a revisal of Lee's draft by Dickinson. In Adams' Diary (*Works*, 11., 366) it appears that he and Henry were in consultation over the Petition, and it is plain that all the papers of the Continental Con-gress, though of necessity written by one man, were the combined logic and opinions of the committee, and the honor belongs to no individual member.

14. The / Petition / of the / Continental Congress / to the / King. And / General Gage's Letter / to the Honorable / Peyton Randolph, Esq; / In Answer to one wrote by the Con-gress. / Philadelphia : / Printed by William and Thomas Bradford, / at the London Coffee-House. / MDCCLXXV. / 8°. pp. (2), [133-] 144.

Same as No. 13 with the addition of a title-page.

15. The / Petition / of the / Grand American Continental / Congress, / to the / King's / Most Excellent Majesty. / America. / Boston, Printed and sold at the / Printing-Office, near the Mill-Bridge. 16°. pp. 8. M.

Oct. 27. Extracts from the Journal.

16. Extracts / From the / Votes and Proceed-ings / Of the American Continental / Congress, / Held at Philadelphia on the / 5th of September 1774. / Containing / The Bill of Rights, A List

4

of Griev-/ances, Occasional Resolves, the / Association, an Address to the People / of Great-Britain, and a Memorial /to the Inhabitants of the British / American Colonies. / Published by order of the Congress. / Philadelphia: / Printed by William and Thomas Bradford, / October 27th, M,DCC,LXXIV.   8°.   pp. (4), 12, 11, 36. P.L.

17.   8°. pp. (4), 23, 36. P.L.

18.   8°. pp. (4), 11, 50. P.

19.   8°. pp. (4), 23, 50. P.H.S.

The first collation given is, I believe, the first edition of this famous pamphlet, being "made up," apparently from the remainders of Nos. 2 and 5, with the addition of the Bill of Rights and List of Grievances. The Letter to the Inhabitants of Quebec (No. 7), though printed after this was issued, and having a separate title is intended to be a part of the "Extracts."

Nothing perhaps shows more thoroughly the intense interest with which the proceedings of the Congress were awaited, than the following list of editions:—

20.   Extracts / from the / Votes and Proceedings / of the American / Continental / Congress, / Held at Philadelphia, September 5, 1774, / Containing / The Bill of Rights, a List of Grievances, Occasional Resolves, the Association, an / Address to the People of Great-Britain, / A Memorial to the Inhabitants of the / British American Colonies, and a Petition / to the King / To which is added, / The Proceedings of the / Provincial Convention, / Held at Philadelphia, January 23, 1775. / Published by order of the Provincial Convention. / Philadelphia: / Printed by William and Thomas Bradford, / at the London Coffee-House. / M,DCC,LXXV.
8°. pp. 80. P.H.S.

21.   Extracts / From the / Votes and Proceedings / Of the American Continental / Congress, / Held at Philadelphia on the / 5th of September, / 1774. / Containing / The Bill of Rights, a List of Griev-/ances, Occasional Resolves, the Asso-/ciation, an Address to the People of / Great-Britain, and a Memorial to / the Inhabitants of the British / American Colonies. / Published by Order of the Congress. / Philadelphia: Printed. / Boston : / Re-Printed by Edes and Gill, in Queen street, / and T. and J. Fleet, in Cornhill. / M.DCC,LXXIV.   8°. pp. 49. M.

22.   8°. pp. 56. C.

The second issue contains the "Suffolk Resolutions," the "Letter to the Inhabitants of Quebec," and several minor resolutions, which were not included in the previous editions.

23.   Extracts / from the / Votes and Proceedings / Of the American Continental / Congress, / Held at Philadelphia on the / 5th of September, / 1774. / Containing / The Bill of Rights, a List of Grievan-/ces, Occasional Resolves, the Association, an / Address to the People of Great-Britain. / and a Memorial to the Inhabitants of the / British American Colonies. / Published by Order of the Congress / Philadelphia, Printed :/ Boston, Re-printed: And sold by John Boyle / in Marlborough-Street, and Mills and Hicks in / School-Street. 1774.   8°. pp. 43. P.L.

24.   8°. pp. 52. M.

The second issue contains the "Letter to the Inhabitants of Quebec."

25.   + Philadelphia, Printed : Boston, Re-printed: And sold by John Boyle, in Marlborough-Street, and Mills and Hicks in School-Street, and Cox and Berry in King Street. 1774. 8°. pp. 43
Title from Stevens's *Nuggets*, No. 1031.

26.   Extracts / from the / Votes and Proceedings / of the / American Continental / Congress, / held at / Philadelphia. / On the 5th of September, 1774. / Containing / The Bill of Rights, a List of Grievances, / Occasional Resolves, the Association, an Address / to the People of Great-Britain, and a Memorial to / the Inhabitants of the British American Colonies. / Published by Order of the Congress. / Phila-delphia: Printed. / Hartford: Re-printed by Eben. Watson, near / the Great-Bridge.
8°. pp. 48. P.L.

Includes the "Letter to the Inhabitants of Quebec."

27.   Extracts / from the / Votes and Proceedings / of the / American Continental / Congress. / held at Philadelphia, / on the Fifth of September. 1774 / Containing, / The Bill of Rights, a List of Grievances, Occasional / Resolves, the Association, an Address to the People / of Great-Britain, and a Memorial to the Inhabitants / of the British American Colonies./ Published by order of the Congress. / Philadelphia printed. / London : Reprinted for J. Almon, opposite / Burlington House, Picca-dilly. / MDCCLXXIV.   8°. pp. (4), 82. B.A.

28.   8°. pp. (4), 59, (1). P.L.

There is a slight variation in the lining of two lines between these two editions, the second being "An Address to the / People of Great Britain and a Memorial to the / Inhabitants of the British American Colonies."

29.   Extracts / from the / Votes and Proceedings / of the / American Continental / Congress./ Held at Philadelphia on the 5th of September 1774. / Containing / The Bill of Rights, a List of Grievances, Occasional Resolves, / the Association, an Address to the People of Great-Britain, / a Memorial to the Inhabitants of the British American / Colonies. and an Address to the Inhabitants of the Province of / Quebec. / Published by Order of the Congress. / New-London : / Printed and sold by Timothy Green. 1774./   4°. pp. 70. B.A.

30.   Extracts / From the Votes and Proceedings / Of the American Continental / Congress, / Held at Philadelphia, / On the 5th of September, 1774. / Containing, / The Bill of Rights, a List of Grievances, Occasional Resolves, the Asso-ciation, an / Address to the People of Great-Britain, Memo-/rial to the Inhabitants of the British American / Colonies, and an Address to the Inhabitants of / Quebec / Published by order of the Congress. / New-London : / Printed by Timothy Green, M, DCC,LXXIV. 4°. pp. 70. P.L.

31.   Extracts / from the / Votes and Proceedings / of the / American Continental Congress, / Held at Philadelphia, / on the 5th of September, 1774. / Containing / The Bill of Rights, / A List of Grievances, / Occasional Resolves, / The Association. / An Address to the Peo-/ple of Great-Britain, / And a Memorial to the / Inhabitants of the / British American / Colonies. / Published by Order of the Congress. / Philadelphia, Printed: / Newport, Rhode Island. / Reprinted and sold by S. Southwick, in Queen-Street, 1774.
8°. pp. 59. P.L.

32.   Extracts / from the / Votes and Proceedings / of the / American / Continental Congress, / held / At Philadelphia, 5th September, 1774. / Containing / The Bill of Rights, a List of Grievances, occasional / Resolves, the

Association, an Address to the / People of Great-Britain, and a Memorial to the / Inhabitants of the British American Colonies. / Published by order of the Congress. / New-York. / Printed by H. Gaine, at the Bible and Crown in / Hanover-Square. / M DCC LXXIV. 12º. pp. 59. **N.**

33. Extracts / from the / Votes and Proceedings / Of the American Continental / Congress, / Held at Philadelphia on the / 5th of September, 1774. / Containing / The Bill of Rights, a List of Grievances, Occasional / Resolves, the Association, an Address to the People of / Great-Britain, and a Memorial to the Inhabitants of the / British American Colonies. / Published by Order of the Congress. / Philadelphia : Printed. / New-York : Reprinted by John Holt, in Dock Street. 4º. pp. 25. **N., P.L.**

Some copies have 7 additional pages, containing No. 8.

33ª. / Containing / The Bill of Rights, A List of Grievan-/ces Ocasional [sic] Resolves, the Associa-/tion, an Address to the People of / Great-Britain, and a Memorial to the / Inhabitants of British American / Colonies. / The Second Edition, to which is added Minutes of the Journal. / Published by Order of the Congress. / Philadelphia : printed. / New-York : Reprinted by John Holt in Dock-Street. [1775.]
8º. pp. 96. **N.**

The same as No. 40, lacking the preliminary four pages.

34. Extracts / from / The Votes and Proceedings of / the / American / Continental / Congress, / Held at Philadelphia, Sept. 5, 1774./ Containing, / The Bill of Rights, a List of Grievances, occasional Resolves, / The Association, an Address to the People of Great Britain,/ and a Memorial to the Inhabitants of the British American / Colonies. / Published by order of the Congress. / Together with / An Address to the Inhabitants of Quebec. / to which are added, / the Resolve of the County of Suffolk, in the Province of Mass-/achusetts-Bay, on the 8th of September, 1774; / with / A Letter from the County Delegates to General Gage, con / cerning the Fortifications upon Boston Neck, and Unanimous / Resolves of the Grand Continental Congress, approving of their / Wisdom and Fortitude; and recommending a perseverance in their firm and / temperate Conduct. / New-York : / Printed for James Rivington, 1774. /
8º. pp. 36. **N.**

35. Extracts / from the / Votes and Proceedings / of the / American Continental / Congress, / Held at Philadelphia on the fifth day of September, / M DCC LXXIV. / Containing, / The Bill of Rights, A List of Grievances, / Occasional Resolves, The Association, An Ad-/ dress to the People of Great-Britain, and a / Memorial to the Inhabitants of the British / American Colonies. / Published by Order of the Congress. / Philadelphia : Printed. / Norwich : Re-printed by Robertsons and / Trumbull, M,DCC.LXXIV./ 8º. pp. 41. **My.H.S.**

36. .....Providence [John Carter] 1774.

Title from Thomas and Haven.

37. Extracts / from the / Votes and Proceedings / of the American Continental / Congress, / Held at Philadelphia / on the / 5th of September 1774. / Williamsburg : Printed by Alexander Purdie and John Dixon. / M.DCC.LXXIV. 8º. **C.**

38. Auszüge / aus den / Stimmungen / und / Verhandlungen / des / Amerikanischen / Congresses / vom besten Lande, / (Gehalten zu Philadelphia, den 5ten Sept. 1774. / Enthaltend / die Bill der Rechten, eine Liste von Be- / schwerden gelegentliche Schlüsse, eine / Adresse an des Volk von Großbrit- / tannien, und ein Memorial an die Ein- / wohner der Brittisch-Amerikanischen / Colonien. / Herausgegeben auf Befehl des Congresses ; / und aus dem Englischen übersetzt. / Philadelphia, / Gedruckt und zu haben bey Henrich Miller. / 1774. / 16º. pp. 76. **P.H.S.** Journal.

39. Journal / of the / Proceedings / of the / Congress, / Held at Philadelphia, / September 5, 1774. / Philadelphia : / Printed by William and Thomas Bradford, at the London Coffee-House. / M,DCC,LXXIV. / 8º. pp. (4), 144. **B.A., P.**

Some copies were issued before pp. 133-144 were printed.

" The rare *original edition*, with the emblematical device on the title, twelve hands sustaining a column resting on Magna Charta and surmounted by the cap of Liberty." —J. H. TRUMBULL.

40. The / Whole Proceedings / of the / American Continental / Congress, / Held at Philadelphia on the / 5th of September, 1774. / Containing / 1. Extracts from the Votes and Proceedings, made, and published by their / Order. / 2. Journal, or Minutes, and Formalities / of their Proceedings, List of Dele-/gates, with their Powers, &c. / Re-printed from the Copies published by Order of / the Congress. / Philadelphia : Printed. / New-York : Reprinted by John Holt, in / Water Street. 1775.
8º. pp. (4), 96. **N.**

41. Journal / of the / Proceedings / of the / Congress, / Held at Philadelphia, September 5th, 1774. / Containing / the Bill of Rights ; a List of Grievances ; / Occasional Resolves ; The Association ; An / Address to the People of Great Britain ; A / Memorial to the Inhabitants of the British / American Colonies ; and, An Address to / the Inhabitants of the Province of Quebec. / Published by Order of the Congress. / To which is added / (Being now first printed by Authority) / An Authentic Copy / of the / Petition to the King. / London : / Printed for J. Almon, opposite Burlington-House, in / Piccadilly / M.DCC LXXV. / 8º. pp. (2), 66, (2). **C.**

In spite of the statement on the title-page, this volume contains none, (the Petition to the King excepted), of the papers there mentioned.

" The late pamphlet, entitled, ' Extracts from the Votes and Proceedings of the American Continental Congress,' contained only a Part of the Journal of that Congress. The whole Journal has since been published in America ; but it was thought proper to reprint only such parts in this Pamphlet, as were omitted in the former, in order that those Gentlemen who have purchased the ' Extracts ' may make their Copies complete, if they chuse it. The two pamphlets contain the entire Journal of the Proceedings of the Congress."

" Dr. Franklin, about the 15th or 16th of Dec. 1774, received these Proceedings of the Congress, with the Petition to the King dated the 26th October previous. The times were growing very serious, and it was thought best to let Almon publish them immediately. The effect was startling, for the pamphlet proclaimed to the discriminating British public (if there was at that time such a body) that the English language had acquired new vigour and clearness in being transplanted to the Western shores. The pith, point and soundness of these public papers astonished the statesmen and confounded the politicians, and at the same time delighted the friends of the Colonies, particularly Lord Chatham and Lord Camden."— HENRY STEVENS.

42. / London : / Printed for E. and C. Dilly / M.DCC.LXXV. 8º. pp. (2), 66, (2), **C.**

6

1775.

May 29 and June 1. Address to Canada.

43. Lettre / Addressée / Aux Habitans / Opprimés de la Province / de / Québec. / De la part du Congrès Général de l'Amérique Sep- / tentrionale, tenu à Philadelphie. [Philadelphia: Fleury Mesplet. 1775.] S°. pp. 7. **P.**

Drafted by Jay, Samuel Adams and Deane. 1,000 copies printed, (with the addition of the resolve of June 1st) for distribution in Canada.

June 12. Resolve for a Fast-day.

44. In Congress, / Monday, June 12, 1775. / Philadelphia: Printed by William and Thomas Bradford. [1775.] / F°. Broadside.

Drafted by Hooper, John Adams and Paine.

45. In Congress, / Monday, June 12, 1775. F°. Broadside. **S.D.**

June 12. Address to Canada and Resolve for Fast-day.

46. In Congress, June 12, 1775 / [Philadelphia:] Printed by John Dunlap [1775.] / F°. Broadside.

The English edition of the Address to Canada, with the resolve making July 20 a day of " Humiliation, Fasting and Prayer." See Nos. 43 and 44.

June 30. Rules for Troops.

47. Rules / and / Articles, / for the better / Government / of the / Troops / Raised, or to be raised, and kept in pay by and at / the joint Expence of the / Twelve united English Colonies / of / North-America. / Philadelphia: / Printed by William and Thomas Bradford, 1775. / 8°. pp. 16. **C, P.**

Prepared by Washington, Schuyler, Deane, Cushing and Hewes. See No. 63.

48. + Philadelphia, Printed: / New York. Reprinted by Hugh Gaine 1775. 8°. pp. 16.

July 6. Declaration to Army.

49. A / Declaration / by the / Representatives / of the / United Colonies / of / North America, / now met in / General Congress / at Philadelphia, / Seting [sic] forth the Causes and Necessity of their / taking up / Arms. / Philadelphia: / Printed by William and Thomas Bradford, 1775 / 8°. pp. (2), 13. **P.**

The committee appointed to prepare this Declaration, consisting of John Rutledge, William Livingston, Franklin, Jay and Johnson, reported a draft on June 24, which, not being approved by the Congress, was recommitted, and Jefferson and Dickinson added to the Committee. "On the 24th, a committee which had been appointed to prepare a declaration of the causes of taking up arms, brought in their report (drawn I believe by J. Rutledge) which not being liked, the House recommitted it, on the 26th, and added Mr. Dickinson and myself to the committee.... I prepared a draught of the declaration committed to us. It was too strong for Mr. Dickinson . . . We therefore requested him to take the paper, and put it into a form he could approve. He did so, preparing an entire new statement, and preserving of the former only the last four paragraphs and half of the preceding one. We approved and reported it to Congress, who accepted it." Jefferson's Autobiography. — *Works,* I., 11.

50. * [Reprinted for R. W. Roche by J. Munsell. Albany: 1865]. 4° & 8°. pp. (2), 13, covers.

51. A / Declaration / by the / Representatives / of the / United Colonies / of / North-America, / now met in / General Congress, / at / Philadelphia; / Setting forth the Causes and Necessity of their taking up / Arms. / Newport: Printed by S. Southwick, in / Queen Street, 1775 / 12°. pp. 11. **M.**

52. A / Declaration / By The / Representatives / Of The / United Colonies / Of / North-America, / Now Met In / General Congress / At / Philadelphia, / Setting forth the Causes and Necessity of their / taking up / Arms. / Philadelphia: Printed, / Watertown: / Re-Printed and Sold by Benjamin Edes. / 1775. 8°. pp. 15. **A.A.S., C.**

July 8. Petition to the King.

53. To the Inhabitants of the / Colony of / New York. / ..... / Pierre Van Courtlandt, Chairman / Jan. 9, 1776. / 8°. pp. 7, 8. **N.**

The only separate edition of the second petition to the King I have been able to find. It was printed, (with the addition of a preliminary Address, the Address of the Mayor of London " To the Electors," and a portion of Chatham's Speech) by the New York Committee of Safety " to correct the assertion that the Continental Congress had made no advances."

The committee to prepare the petition consisted of Dickinson, Johnson, John Rutledge, Jay and Franklin; and Dickinson wrote the draft.

July 8. Address to the People of England.

54. The / Twelve United Colonies. / By their Delegates in / Congress. / To the Inhabitants of / Great Britain. / [Philadelphia: W. and T. Bradford. 1775.] S°. pp. 8. **P.**

The committee to prepare the address consisted of R. H. Lee, R. R. Livingston, and Pendleton. Lee wrote the draft, which was preserved for a number of years by the family, but has since been lost.

55. The Twelve United Colonies, / by their Delegates / in / Congress, / to the / Inhabitants / of / Great Britain. / Philadelphia: / Printed by William and Thomas Bradford. / M,DCC.LXXV. 8°. pp. 16.

56. An Address from the Delegates of the Twelve United Colonies, to the People of England. Newport: Printed by S. Southwick in Queen Street, 1775. 8°. pp. 13.

Title from Hammett's *Bibliography of Newport.*

July 15. Partial suspension of Association.

57. [Whereas, the Government of Great Britain hath prohibited the exportation of Arms and Ammunition ..... Resolved ..... Philadelphia: Printed by W. and T. Bradford 1775.] Broadside.

A resolve allowing the exportation of produce to be exchanged for materials of war.

" *Ordered,* That a copy of the above be delivered to the Delegates of the Colony of *Pennsylvania,* who are desired to request the committee of this city to forward the same in handbills to the *West Indies.*" — *Journal.*

July 28. Address to People of Ireland.

58. An / Address / of the / Twelve United Colonies / of / North-America, / By their / Representatives / in / Congress, / To the People of Ireland. / Philadelphia: / Printed by W. and T. Bradford, 1775. / 8°. pp. (2), 10. **P.**

Drafted by Deane, William Livingston, Samuel Adams, R. R. Livingston and Pendleton.

59. ..... Norwich: Printed by Robertson and Trumbull. 1775. 8°.

Title from *Sabin,* No. 35061.

60. ..... New York. Reprinted 1775. 8°. pp. 10.

Title from *Thomas and Haven.*

July 31. Observations on Lord North's Motion.

61. The Several Assemblies of New-Jersey, / Pennsylvania and Virginia, having re- / ferred to the Congress a resolution of the House of / Commons of Great Britain, which resolution / is in

these words : / .... [Philadelphia : W. and T. Bradford. 1775.] 8°. pp. 8. S.D., P., N.

The opinion of the Congress on the resolution, prepared by Franklin, Jefferson, John Adams and Lee. The draft, in his own handwriting, is in the Jefferson Mss. in the Department of State.

Nov. 4. Capitulation of Montreal.

62. Articles / of Capitulation, / Made and entered into between Richard / Montgomery, Esquire, Brigadier Ge- / neral of the Continental Army, and the Citi- / zens and inhabitants of Montreal ..... [Philadelphia] Printed by John Dunlap. [1775.] / F°. Broadside. P.

Nov. 7. Rules for Troops.

63. Rules / and / Articles, / for the better / Government / of the / Troops / Raised, or to be raised, and kept in pay by and at / the joint Expence of the / Thirteen United English Colonies / of North America. / Philadelphia : / Printed by William and Thomas Bradford, 1775./ 8°. pp. 16. P.

A revision of the Rules adopted June 30th (No. 47) with the additional ones adopted November 7. See also No. 107.

64. Rules / and / Articles, / for the Better / Government / of the Troops / Raised, or to be raised, and kept in pay by and / at the joint Expense of the / Twelve united English Colonies / of / North America. / Philadelphia, Printed : / New-York, Re-printed and sold by H. Gaine, / at the Bible and Crown, in Hanover-Square, / M,DCC,LXXV. / 8°. pp. 16. N.

65. Rules and Articles, for the better Government of the Troops Raised, or to be raised and kept in pay by and at the joint Expense of the Twelve United English Colonies of North America. Watertown : Printed by B. Edes. 1775. 8°. pp. 16. A.A.S.

66. Réglement / Militaire / Concernant / La Police / et / La Discipline, / Que doivent observer les Troupes qui sont ou seront / dans la suite levées & payées par les Treize / Colonies Unies de l'Amerique Septentrionale / Traduit de l'Anglaise, Par F. Daymon. / A Philadelphie ; / Chez Fleury Mesplet & Ch. Berger, / Imprimeurs & Libraires. / M.DCC.LXXVI. 8°. pp. 39.

" Resolved, That the articles of war be translated into French, and 500 copies sent to Canada " ......

"To Francis Daymon, for translating into French the rules and articles for the better regulating the Continental troops, the sum of 15½ dollars : To Mons. Mesplet, for printing the military rules, and French letters to the inhabitants of Canada, the sum of 44 dollars :" — *Journal.*

Nov. 24. Intercepted Letters, etc.

67. Extract of a Letter from General Montgo- / mery, dated Camp before St. John's, October 20, 1775 / ..... / Articles proposed for his Majesty's / Garrison at Chambly / ..... / An Account of Stores taken at Chambly. / ..... / A List of Officers taken at Chambly. / ..... / Extract of a Letter from Gen. Montgomery, dated / Camp near St. John's, Nov. 3, 1775. / ..... Articles of Capitulation, proposed by Major Charles / Preston for his Majesty's Fort of St-John's, in / the Province of Canada. / ..... / Extracts of several Letters brought by Capt. / Robbins, in the schooner Two Sisters, lately seized by / an armed vessel in the service of the United Colonies. / Published by Order of Congress. / ..... [Philadelphia : W. & T. Bradford. 1775.] F°. 1 l. S.D.

"The Committee to whom the intercepted Letters were referred brought in their Report ; which being read and agreed to,

Resolved, That it be recommitted to the said Committee, and that they have the extracts agreed to published, together with an authentic account of the capture of *Chambly* and *St. John's,* and to have one thousand copies struck off, to go with the despatches." — *Journal.*

Nov. 28. Rules for Navy.

68. [Rules for the Regulation of the Navy of the United Colonies. Philadelphia : W. and T. Bradford. 1775 ?]

I have been unable to find a copy. See No. 114.

Dec. 6. Declaration.

69. In Congress. / December 6, 1775 / [Philadelphia :] Printed by John Dunlap. [1775.] / F°. Broadside. S.D.

A Declaration by the Congress in answer to the King of Great Britain's Proclamation of August 23, 1775.

Extracts from the Journal.

70. Extracts / from the / Proceedings of the American Continental / Congress, / Held at Philadelphia, on the Tenth Day of May, 1775. / Containing, An Address to the People of Ireland, an Ad- / dress to the Lord-Mayor of London, and the Opi- / nion of Congress on the boasted conciliatory Plan offered by Administration in Parliament, February / 20, 1775. / Providence / Printed by John Carter, at Shakespear's Head [1775.] / 8°. pp. 22. P.L.

See also No. 77.

71. A / Declaration / by the / Representatives of the United / Colonies of North-America, / Now met in General Congress at / Philadelphia ; / setting forth the Causes and Necessity / of their taking up Arms. / Also, / An Address / from the / Twelve United Colonies, / By their Delegates in Congress, to the / Inhabitants of Great-Britain. / Philadelphia, printed by W. and Thomas Bradford, / and Bristol reprinted by W. Pine, 1775. / (Price Two-Pence.) 16°. pp. 16. C.

72. The / Declaration / by the / Representatives / of the / United Colonies of North America, / now met in General Congress at Philadelphia, / Setting forth the / Causes and Necessity of taking up Arms. / The / Letter of the Twelve United Colonies / by their Delegates in Congress to the Inhabitants of Great Britain, / Their Humble Petition to his Majesty, / and / Their Address to the People of Ireland. / Collected together for the Use of Serious Thinking Men, / By Lovers of Peace. / Read with Candour : Judge with Impartiality. / London : / Printed in the Year, MDCCLXXV. 8°. pp. 32. C.

73. An die | Einwohner von Irland, | von | den Abgeordneten der Vereinigten Colonien | Newhampchire, Massachusetts = Bay, Rhode = | Eyland und Providenz, Connecticut, Neu= | york, New=Jersey, Pennsylvanien, der | Niedern Grafschaften an der Delaware, | Maryland, Virginien, Nord= und Süd= | Carolina, im General=Congreß zu Phila= | phia, [sic] den 16ten May, 1775. | Nebst der | Meinung des General = Congresses, | betreffend | Einen Entschluß des Hauses der Ge= | meinen von Großbrittannien, | vom 20sten Fe= | bruary, 1775. | Philadelphia, | gedruckt und zu bekommen bey Henrich Miller, in | der Rees=straße, 1775. 16°. pp. 16.

Journal. May to July.

74. Journal / of the / Proceedings / of the / Congress, / held at / Philadelphia. May 10, 1775. / Philadelphia: / Printed and Sold by William and Thomas / Bradford, at the London Coffee-House. / M.DCC.LXXV./ 8°. pp (4), iv, 239. **P.H.S.**

75. Journal / of the / Proceedings / of the / Congress, / held at / Philadelphia, / May 10, 1775. / Wilmington, / Printed by James Adams, in High-street, 1776. 8°. pp. 10. **H.**

76. Journal / of the/Proceedings/of the/Congress, / held at / Philadelphia. / May 10, 1775. / Published by Order of the Congress. / Philadelphia: Printed; / London: Re-printed for J. Almon, opposite / Burlington-House in Piccadilly, 1776. 8°. pp. (4), 200, (8). **C.**

77. Extracts / from the / Votes and Proceedings / of the / American / Continental Congress, / held / At Philadelphia, 10th May, 1775 / Published by Order of Congress. / New-York :/ Printed and Sold by John Anderson, / at Beekman's-Slip. / M.DCC.LXXV. 8°. pp. (2), 192.
    Though this is called "Extracts," it is really the entire Journal.

Journal. Sept. to Dec.

78. Journal / of the Congress, / of the / United States / of / America; / Continued. / Philadelphia: / Printed and Sold, by William and Thomas / Bradford, at the Coffee-House. / M.DCC.LXXVI. 8°. pp. (4), 218. **P.H.S.**

Journal. 1774-1775.

79. Journals / of / Congress. / Containing the / Proceedings from Sept. 5, 1774, to Jan. 1, 1776. Published by order of Congress. / Volume I. / Philadelphia : / Printed and sold by R. Aitken, Bookseller, Front-street. / M.DCC.LXXVII. 8°. pp. (2), 310, (12). **B.A., N., C.** 163
    See note to No. 163.
    This is the first volume of the official edition, issued at the end of each year. I shall give each volume under the year at which the proceedings end, as they were practically separate works; but I shall also give a title and collation of the whole series, together with those of the reprints of 1800 and 1823, in the collected works, at the end of this list.

Members of the Congress.

80. A List of the Delegates who attended the Congress, / held at Philadelphia, May 10, 1775. [Philadelphia :? 1775.] / 8°. Broadside. **P.L.**

Method of making Salt-Petre.

81. Several Methods / of Making / Salt-Petre ; / recommended to the / Inhabitants / of the / United Colonies. / by their / Representatives / In Congress, / Philadelphia : / Printed by W. and T. Bradford. 1775. / 8°. pp. 12. **P.**

82. Several methods / of making / salt-petre ;/ recommended to the / inhabitants / of the / United Colonies. / By the / Honorable / Continental Congress. / And / Re-published by Order of the / General Assembly / of the / Colony of Massachusetts-Bay, / Together with the resolve of said Assembly. / and / An appendix, / By Doctor William Whiting. / Watertown : / Printed and Sold by Benjamin Edes, near the Bridge, / 1775. 8°. pp. 20. **B.A.**

Rates of Postage of Continental Post-Office.

83. Tables / Of the Port of all Single Letters carried by Post in the Northern District of North America, / As Established by / Congress. / One Thousand Seven Hundred and Seventy-five. / ..... / [Signed] B. Franklin, / Post Master General. / [Philadelphia : 1775?] F°. Broadside. **S.D.**

Directions for keeping Post Office Accounts.

84. Directions to the Deputy Post-Masters, for keeping their accounts.....[signed] B. Franklin. F°. Broadside. **P.H.S.**

1776.

January 24. Address to Canada.

85. Aux / Habitants / De la Province du Canada. / [Philadelphia :] Chez Fleury Mesplet & Charles Berger [1776]. F°. Broadside. **P.**
    Drafted by Livingston, Lynch, and Wilson. The English original is printed in Force's *Archives*, 4, iv, 1653. See note to No. 66.

86. Aux Habitants / De la Province du Canada. [Philadelphia : Mesplet & Berger. 1776.] F°. Broadside.

February 19. Oration on Montgomery.

87. An / Oration / In Memory of / General Montgomery. / and of the / Officers and Soldiers, / Who Fell with Him, December 31, 1775, / before / Quebec ; / Drawn up (and Delivered February 19. 1776.)/ At the Desire of the / Honorable Continental Congress. / By William Smith, D.D. / Provost of the College and Academy / Of Philadelphia. / ..... / Philadelphia : / Printed by John Dunlap, in Market-Street. / M,DCC,LXXVI./ 8°. pp. (6), 44. **P.H.S.**
    "The oration was an insolent performance. A motion was made to thank the orator, and ask a copy, but opposed with great spirit and vivacity from every part of the room, and at last withdrawn, lest it should be rejected, as it certainly would have been, with indignation. The orator then printed it himself, after leaving out or altering some offensive passages."—*Familiar Letters of John Adams*, 167.

88. ..... New York : 1776. 8°. pp.

89. ...... Philadelphia, Printed; / London, / Reprinted for J. Almon.....MDCCLXXVI. 8°. pp. iv, 36. **B.A.**

90. * Philadelphia, Printed : / Newcastle, Reprinted by T. Robson and Co. And sold at their Printing-Office. 8°. pp. 35. **P.L.**

91. * Philadelphia, Printed : / Newport : Reprinted by Solomon Southwick. / M,DCC,LXXVI./ 8°. pp. (2), 30. **P.L.**

92. ..... Norwich, Conn. John Trumbull. 1776. 8°.

March 16. Proclamation for a fast.

93. In Congress, / Saturday, March 16, 1776./ Philadelphia : Printed by John Dunlap. [1776]. F°. Broadside. **P.**
    Prepared and introduced, with the permission of Congress, by William Livingston.

94. A Proclamation for a Continental Fast. / In Congress, Saturday, March 16, 1776. / [Boston : 1776?] F°. Broadside. **M.**

March 23. Resolutions concerning privateers.

95. In Congress, / March 23, 1776. / Philadelphia : Printed by John Dunlap. [1776]. F°. Broadside. **S.D., P.H.S.**
    See No. 97.

March 27. Sermon on Ward.

96. Death, the last Enemy, destroyed by Christ. / A / Sermon, / Preached, March 27,

1776, / before / The Honorable / Continental Congress; / on the Death of / The Honorable / Samuel Ward, Esq. / one of the / Delegates from the Colony / of Rhode Island, / who died of the Small-Pox, in this city, / (Philadelphia) / March 26, Æt. 52. / Published at the desire of many who heard it. / By Samuel Stillman, M.A. / Philadelphia: / Printed by Joseph Crukshank, in Market-street. / MDCCLXXVI.

8°. pp. 28.

April 3. Additional resolutions concerning privateers.

97. In Congress, April 3, 1776.

F°. Broadside. N.

See No. 95.

May 6. Instructions to commanders of American Vessels.

98. In Congress, May 6, 1776. F°. Broadside.

May 15. Resolution concerning state governments.

99. In Congress / May 15, 1776. / Philadelphia : Printed by John Dunlap. [1776].

F°. Broadside. P.

The resolve of May 10, with the preamble, drafted by John Adams, John Rutledge, and R. H. Lee, adopted May 15. The resolve was written by John Adams.

100. In Congress, May 15, 1776. [Dresden: Judah Padock & Alden Spooner? 1777.]

F°. Broadside. S.D.

With a letter from Thomas Young and a note from "Your Committee" dated April 12, 1777, relative to Vermont's position toward the Continental Congress. See *Journal*, June 28, 1777.

July 4. Declaration of Independence.

101. In Congress, July 4, 1776. / A Declaration by the Representatives of the United States / of America, in General Congress Assembled. [Philadelphia: John Dunlap. 1776.]

F°. Broadside.

I judge this to be the first edition of this famous paper, as it is the one gummed into the MS. Journals of Congress by the Secretary.

Thomas Jefferson, John Adams, Benjamin Franklin, Roger Sherman, and Robert R. Livingston were appointed June 11 by Congress to prepare the declaration. Jefferson, at the request of the committee, wrote the first draft, which was slightly altered by Adams and Franklin, and in that form accepted by the committee, who reported it to Congress June 28; where, after debate and amending, it was adopted July 4. A facsimile of Jefferson's rough draft, showing the corrections made by Adams and Franklin, is printed in the Charlottesville and Boston editions of his "Memoirs," as edited by T. J. Randolph, and in the first issue of his "Writings," edited by H. A. Washington:—A facsimile of a fair copy, in Jefferson's handwriting, is printed in volume III of the "Papers of James Madison":—A copy showing the amendments made by Congress, in comparison with the original draft, is contained in all the editions of Jefferson's "Memoirs" and "Writings." In 1824 Congress ordered 200 copies to be reproduced in facsimile on parchment, of the engrossed copy, and this plate was used later to print that contained in Force's *Archives* (v. 1., 1595), and has also been used to print a separate edition on paper. Both Jefferson's draft and the engrossed copy have been reproduced in facsimile many times, and there have been many printed editions, besides the contemporary editions noted herein. In the Adams Mss. is a copy of Jefferson's draft, in the writing of Adams, made before even Jefferson had made his corrections and interlineations.

102. In Congress, July 4, 1776. / Declaration / By the Representatives of the / United States of America. / In General Congress assembled. / ..... / Philadelphia : Printed by John Dunlap.

F°. Broadside. S.D.

103. In / Congress, / July 4, 1776 / A Declaration / By the / Representatives / of the / United States of America, / In General Congress assembled /..... / Salem, Massachusetts-Bay: Printed [by Ezekiel Russell?] F°. Broadside. M.

104. In Congress, July 4, 1776 / Declaration / By the Representatives of the / United States of America / In General Congress Assembled.

F°. Broadside.

Measures 15 X 19½ inches.

105. In Congress, July 4, 1776. / The unanimous Declaration / of the / Thirteen United States of America. /...../ Baltimore, in Maryland: Printed by Mary Katherine Goddard./ [1777.] F°. B. BPL.

The first edition of the Declaration printed for the Congress was issued before it was engrossed on parchment, and signed. It was therefore merely signed by Hancock, and attested by Thomson. This edition was printed for the Congress "with the list of the several members of Congress subscribed thereto," to be filed in the archives of each state.

July 12. First draft of Articles of Confederation.

106. Articles / of / Confederation and Perpetual Union / Between the Colonies of / New Hampshire, / The Counties of New-Castle, Massachusetts-Bay, Kent and Sussex on Delaware,

Rhode-Island,	Maryland,
Connecticut,	Virginia,
New-York,	North-Carolina,
New-Jersey,	South-Carolina, and
Pennsylvania,	Georgia.

..... [Philadelphia : 1776.] F°. pp. 8. S.D.

Drafted by a committee, of one from each state. The original draft is in the handwriting of John Dickinson.

"Ordered, That eighty copies, and no more, of the confederation, as brought in by the committee, be immediately printed, and be deposited with the secretary, who shall deliver one copy to each member.

That the printer be under oath to deliver all the copies, which he shall print, together with the copy-sheet to the secretary." —*Journal.*

July 19. Resolve concerning volunteers.

107. In Congress, July 19, 1776 [Philadelphia : 1776]. 4°. pp. (3). P.H.S.

"A resolution recommending the Convention of Pennsylvania to hasten the March of the Associates into New Jersey, with order of the date from the Convention to the Colonel or Commanding Officer of the Battalion of the County of ——." —*Hildeburn.*

July 20. Plan of Treaties.

108. (1) There shall be a firm, inviolable, and universal peace, and a true and / sincere friendship between A. and B. and the subjects of A. and B..... / ..... [Philadelphia : 1776].

F°. pp. 5. S.D.

"Resolved, That the committee to prepare a plan of treaties to be proposed to foreign powers, consist of five: The members chosen, Mr. Dickinson, Mr. Franklin, Mr. J. Adams, Mr. Harrison, and Mr. R. Morris.......

Resolved, That the plan of treaties be printed for the use of the members, under the restrictions and regulations prescribed for printing the plan of confederation; [see No. 106] and that, in the printed copy, the names of persons, places and states, be omitted." —*Journal.*

Reprinted in the *Secret Journals*, ii, 7, and in Force's *Archives*, v. 1., 1344. The plan was drafted by Adams: see his *Works*, ii., 516.

August 14. Specimen of Journal.

109. Journal of Congress / Wednesday, August 14, 1776. [Philadelphia : Charles Cist. 1785.] F°. 1 l. S.D.

A specimen sheet, printed by Cist to accompany his proposals for printing the Journal.

August 20. Second draft of Articles of Confederation.

110. Articles / of / Confederation and Perpetual Union / Between the Colonies of / New-Hampshire, / The Counties of New-Castle, Massachusetts-Bay, Kent and Sussex on Delaware,

Rhode-Island,	Maryland,
Connecticut,	Virginia,
New-York,	North-Carolina,
New-Jersey,	South-Carolina, and
Pennsylvania,	Georgia.

..... [Philadelphia : 1776.] F°. pp. 6. S.D.

Printed under the same restrictions as the first draft, No. 106. See No. 151.

September 20. Revised Articles of War.

111. Rules / and / Articles / for the better / Government / of the / Troops / Raised, or to be raised and kept in pay by / and at the expence of the United/States of America. / Philadelphia :/ Printed by John Dunlap, in Market-Street. / M.DCC.LXXVI. 8°. pp. 36. C., M., P., N.

112. Rules and Articles for the better Government of the Troops raised, or to be raised. and kept in Pay, by and at the Expence of the United States of America. In Congress, September 20, 1776. . . . [Philadelphia? 1776?] 12°. pp. 25. Title from Sabin.

113. Rules / and / Articles / for the better Government / of the / Troops / Raised, or to be raised and kept in pay / by and at the expence of the Uni- / ted States of / America. / Philadelphia, Printed : Fisk-Kill, / Re-printed by S. London. M.DCC.LXXVI. / 12°. pp. 31.

114. The Rules and Articles of War, For the Government of the Troops of the United States. Extracted from the Journals of Congress for the year 1776. Baltimore : Printed by Philip Edwards. MDCCXCIV. 8°. pp. 28.

October 3. Resolve to borrow $5,000,000.

115. In Congress, / October 3, 1776. [Philadelphia :] Printed by John Dunlap [1776]. F°. Broadside. P.

Oct. 21. Oath of Allegiance.

116. I / do acknowledge the United States of Ame-/rica to be Free, Independent and Sovereign States, ... / [Philadelphia? 1776.] 16°. Broadside. P.L.

Nov. 18. U. S. Lottery.

116.* United States Lottery No. / Class the first. / This Ticket entitles the Bearer to receive / such Prize... / [Philadelphia 1776]. Min. Broadside. P.L.

December 10. Address to the people.

117. The Representatives of the United States of / America, in Congress assembled, / To the People in General, and particularly to the Inhabitants / of Pennsylvania, and the adjacent States. [Philadelphia : 1776.] F°. Broadside. P.

Drafted by Witherspoon, R. H. Lee and J. Adams.

118. Die Repräsentanten der Vereinigten Staaten | von America, im Congreß versammelt, | An das Volk überhaupt und an die Einwohner Pennsylvaniens | und

der angrenzenden Staaten insbesondere. | [Philadelphia : Henrich Miller. 1776.] F°. Broadside.

December 11. Resolution for a Fast.

119. [Resolved. that it be recommended to all the United States, as soon as possible, to appoint a day of solemn fasting and humiliation.....]

Prepared by the same committee who prepared the address of December 10. I have not traced a copy of the Philadelphia edition.

120. In Congress. December 11, 1776 / .... / Hartford : Reprinted by Ebenezer Watson. F°. 1 l.

Extracts from Journal relative to marine affairs.

121. Extract / from the / Journals of Congress, / relative to the / Capture and Condemnation of Prizes, / and the / Fitting out Privateers; / together with the / Rules and Regulations of the Navy, / And Instructions to the / Commanders of Private Ships of War. / Philadelphia : / Printed by John Dunlap, / M.DCC.LXXVI. 8°. pp. (2), 45. P.H.S.

122. Extract uit de Dag-Registers van het Noord-Amerikaansche Congres, Betrekklyk tot het neemen en verbeurdverklaaren van Scheeps-Ordonnantiën en Schikkingen der Zee-Vloot, en de Pryzen en het intrusten van Kaapers ; benevens de Instructiën voor de Bevelhebbers der Particuliere Oorlogschepen. Philadelphia. 1777. 8°. pp. 48. Title from Sabin. No. 13510.

Journal. Sept., 1775, to April, 1776.

123. Journal / of the / Proceedings of Congress / Held at Philadelphia. / From September 5, 1775, to April 30, 1776. / Philadelphia : Printed ; / London : Reprinted for J. Almon, opposite / Burlington-House. Piccadilly / M.DCC.LXXVIII. 8°. pp. 202. C., N.

Journal. January to May, 1776.

124. The / Journals / of the / Proceedings / of / Congress. / Held at Philadelphia. / From January to May, 1776. / Philadelphia : / Printed by R. Aitken, Bookseller, opposite the / London Coffee-house, Front-Street. / M.DCC.LXXVI / 8°. P.H.S.

"Collation : Title, 1 leaf; Journal for January, pp. 1-94; Title, 1 leaf; Journal for February, pp. 1-70; Title, 1 leaf; Journal for March, pp. 71-146; Journal for April, pp. 147-247. The second title is : The / Journals / of / Congress / For February, 1776. / Philadelphia : / Printed and sold by R. Aitken, Front-Street. / M.DCC.LXXVI. / This edition appears to have been issued in monthly parts. Aitken says of it, 'I was ordered (in April 1776) to print no more in this large type, and to begin a new edition beginning the session of Congress, which rendered the sale of the above abortive, meantime, I sold 80 copies. I also sold 14 reams of this edition to Benjamin Flower, for the use of the army for cartridges at 30s. per ream.'" — Hildeburn.

Journal. 1776.

125. Journals / of / Congress. / Containing / the / Proceedings / From January 1, 1776, to January 1, 1777. / Published by order of Congress. / Volume II. / York-Town : [Pennsylvania] / Printed by John Dunlap. / M DCC.LXXII. 8°. (2), 520, xxvii. B.A., N., C.

Feb. 17. Advertisement for Seamen.

126. [Advertisement of the Continental Navy Board for Seamen. Philadelphia. Robert Aitken. 1777.]

This and Nos. 128, 131, 136, and 148 are taken from Hildeburn's Issues of the Press in Pennsylvania (No. 3536). He quotes them from Aitkin's ledger. 300 copies were printed.

Feb. 25. Resolutions on Desertions.

127. [Congress took into consideration the report of the Committee on deserters and thereupon came to the following resolutions.......]

"Order, That the foregoing resolve, and the first, second, and third articles of the 6th section of the Articles of War, be published in the several papers, ... and, also that 300 copies be printed in handbills and sent to camp." *Journal.*

Feb. 26. Letters and Orders for Continental Ships.

128. [Letters and Orders for Continental Vessels, printed for the Continental Navy Board. Philadelphia: Robert Aitken. 1777.]

See Note to No. 126. 250 copies printed.

Feb. 26. Rate of Interest.

129. In Congress, / Baltimore, February 26th, 1777. / ..... / Baltimore: Printed by M. K. Goddard. Fº. Broadside. P.L.

Mar. 25. Returns of Loan Offices.

130. In Congress, / March 25. 1777. [Philadelphia: 1777.] Fº. Broadside. P.L.

Apr. 1. Resolution of Navy Board.

131. [Resolve of the Marine Committee. Philadelphia: Printed by Robert Aitken. 1777.]

See Note to No. 126. 150 copies printed.

Apr. 1. Resolution for Paying Troops.

132. In Congress, / April 1, 1777 / ..... / Printed by John Dunlap. Fº. Broadside. S.D.

Apr. 4. Resolution on Commissary General of Musters.

133. In Congress, / April 4, 1777 / ..... / Printed by John Dunlap. Fº. 1 f.

Apr. 7. Resolution on Continental Hospitals.

134. In Congress, / April 7, 1777 / ..... / Printed by John Dunlap. Fº. 1 f.

135. In Congress, / April 7, 1777. / ..... / Printed by Hall and Sellers. 1779. Fº. 1 f. S.D.

Apr. 11. Resolutions concerning Monopoly.

135¹. In Congress, / April 11, 1777. / ..... / Printed by John Dunlap. Fº. Broadside.

Apr. 12. Rules of Navy Board.

136. [Rules and Regulations of Continental Navy Board. Philadelphia: Printed by R. Aitken. 1777.]

See Note to No. 126. 150 copies printed.

Apr. 14. Resolution on Recruiting.

137. In Congress, / April 14th. 1777. [Philadelphia: 1777.] Fº. Broadside.

Apr. 14. Resolution for Committee of Conference.

138. In Congress. / April 14, 1777. / ..... / John Dunlap. Fº. Broadside. H.S.P.

Apr. 14. Revision of Rules and Articles for Troops.

139. In Congress, April 14th, 1777 / ..... / Philadelphia: Printed by John Dunlap. Fº. Broadside.

141. In Congress, April 14, 1777. [Philadelphia: 1777.] 8º. pp. 2.

Probably printed to add to the already printed editions of the Rules. Thomas Heyward, F. L. Lee, and Abraham Clarke were the revising committee.

142.. [Rules and Articles. Philadelphia? 1777.] 8º. pp. 31, 2.

The copy seen lacked the title-page. I have also seen a copy of what was apparently a New Jersey edition, pp. 30 and more, in the same condition.

143. Rules / and / articles / for the better / government / of the / troops / Raised, or to be raised and kept in pay by / and at the expence of the United / States of / America. / Boston, New-England: / Printed by Benjamin Edes, in Queen-Street. / M,DCC,LXXVII. /

Apr. 29. Resolution on Accounts.

144. In Congress, April 29, 1777 / ..... / Philadelphia, Printed by John Dunlap. Fº. Broadside.

May 14. Resolutions on Quartermaster's Department.

145. In Congress, May 14, 1777. / ..... / Philadelphia, Printed by John Dunlap. Fº. 1 l. S.D.

June 10. Resolutions on Commissary Department.

146. In Congress, June 10, 1777. / ..... / Philadelphia: Printed by John Dunlap in Market Street. Fº. pp. 4. S.D.

July 19. Conduct of the Enemy.

147. [Report of the Committee appointed to enquire into the conduct of the Enemy, with affidavits.]

4,000 copies in English and 2,000 copies in German were ordered " published in a pamphlet " by the Congress, but it is questionable if it ever was done, as no copy is now known to exist. See *Journals*, III, 143, 187.

Aug. 11. Advertisement of Navy Board.

148. [Advertisement for the encouragement of the Navy in the River, by the Continental Navy Board.] 4º.

See note to No. 126. 100 copies printed.

Sept. 6. Report of Treasury Committee.

149. In Congress, September 6, 1777 / ..... / Philadelphia: Printed by John Dunlap. Fº. Broadside. S.D.

Sept. 12. Information from Army.

150. Chad's Ford, Sept. 11, 1777. 5 O'Clock, A.M. / Philadelphia, Printed by John Dunlap. Fº. Broadside.

" Letters from Robert H. Harrison, and General Washington to John Hancock, announcing the loss of the battle of Brandywine." Title and note from Hildeburn's *Issues of the Press in Pennsylvania.* Published by order of Congress.

Nov. 15. Articles of Confederation.

151. Articles / of / Confederation / and / Perpetual Union / between the / States / of / New-Hampshire, Massachusetts-Bay, Rhode- / Island and Providence Plantation, Con-/necticut, New-York, New-Jersey, Pennsyl- / vania, Delaware, Maryland, Virginia, / North-Carolina, South-Carolina, and Georgia. / Lancaster: / Printed by Francis Bailey. / M,DCC,LXXVII. Fº. pp. 26. A.P.S.

152. Articles / of / Confederation / and / Perpetual Union / between the / States / of / New-Hampshire, Massachusetts Bay, / Rhode-Island and Providence Planta-/tions, Connecticut, New-York, New- / Jersey, Pennsylvania, Delaware,

Ma-/ryland, Virginia, North-Carolina, / South-Carolina, and Georgia. / Annapolis: / Printed by Frederick Green [1777]. 8°. pp. 15. **P.L.**

153. Articles / of / Confederation / and / Perpetual Union / between the / States / of / New-Hampshire, Massachusetts-Bay, Rhode-Island / and Providence plantations, Connecticut. New-/ York, New-Jersey, Pennsylvania, Delaware, Mary-/ land, Virginia, North-Carolina, South-Carolina, / and Georgia. / Lancaster. (Pennsylvania) printed: / Boston, Re-printed by John Gill. / Printer to the General Assembly./M.DCC.-LXXVII. F°. pp. 46. **B.A.**

154. Articles / of / Confederation / and / Perpetual Union / between the / States / of / New-Hampshire, Massachusetts-Bay, Rhode-/ Island and Providence Plantations, Con-/necticut, New-York, New-Jersey, Pennsy-/ lvania, Delaware, Maryland, Virginia, / North Carolina, South Carolina, and Georgia. / Exeter, New Hampshire, / Printed by Zechariah Fowle. / M,DCC,-LXXVII. F°. pp. 8.

155. Articles / of / Confederation / and / Perpetual Union / between the / States / of / New-Hampshire, Massachusetts Bay, Rhode Island and Provi-/dence Plantations, Connecticut, New-York, New-Jersey, / Pennsylvania, Delaware, Maryland, Virginia, North Ca- / rolina, South-Carolina, and Georgia. / Lancaster, Printed, / Newbern: Re-printed by James Davis, / MDCC-LXXVII. F°. pp. 9. C.

156. Articles / of / Confederation / and / Perpetual Union / between the / States / of / New-Hampshire, Massachusetts-Bay, Rhode-/ Island and Providence Plantations, Connec-/ticut. New-York, New-Jersey, Pennsylva-/ nia, Delaware, Maryland, Virginia, North-/ Carolina, South-Carolina, and Georgia. / New-London: Printed by Timothy Green, Printer to / the State of Connecticut. / M,DCC,LXXVII. F°. pp. 11. C.

157. Articles de Confédération & d'Union perpétuelles entre les États de Nouvel Hampshire, Baie de Massachusetts, Rhode Island, Connecticut, Nouvelle York, Nouvelle Jersey, Pennsylvanie, Les Comtés de New Castle, Kent & Sussex sur la rivière Delaware, Maryland, Virginie, Caroline Septentrionale, Caroline Méridionale, Georgie, etc., [Philadelphia?] MDCCLXXVII. 8°. pp. 16.

Title from the *Carter Brown Catalogue*.

"That a committee of three be appointed to procure a translation to be made of the articles of Confederation into the French Language ... The members chosen, Mr. Duer, Mr. Lovell, and Mr. F. L. Lee."—*Journal.*

158. Articles / of / Confederation / and / Perpetual Union / between the / States / of / New-Hampshire, Massachusetts-Bay, Rhode-/ Island and Providence Plantations, Con-/necticut, New-York, New Jersey, Pennsyl-/ vania, Delaware, Maryland, Virginia, / North Carolina, South Carolina, and Georgia. / Williamsburg: / Printed by J. Dixon & W. Hunter. / M,DCC, LXXVIII. 4°. pp. 15. C.

159. Articles / of / Confederation / and / Perpetual Union / between the / States / of / New-Hampshire, Massachusetts Bay, Rhode Island, and Providence Plantations, / Connecticut, New York, New Jersey, Pennsylvania, Delaware, Maryland, / Virginia, North Carolina, South Carolina, and Georgia. / Williamsburg : / Printed by Alexander Purdie. F°. 2 l.

161. The / Articles / of Confederation; / the / Declaration of Rights; / the Constitution of this Commonwealth / and the / Articles of the Definitive Treaty / between / Great-Britain and the United / States of America. / Published by Order of the General Assembly / Richmond: / Printed by Dixon and Holt. [1784] 12°. pp. 35. C.

162. Artikel | Des | Bundes | Und der | Immerwährenden | Eintracht | Zwischen der Staaten von | Neu-Hampshire. Massachusets-Bay, | Rhode-Eyland und Providence Plan- | tagen, Connecticut, Neu-York, Neu-Jersey. Pennsylvanien, Delaware, | Maryland, Virginien, Nord-Caro- | lina, Süd-Carolina, und Georgien. | Aus dem En- | glischen Ueberseßt. | Laucaster | Gedruckt und zu haben bey Francis Bailey. | MDCCLXXVII . | 16mo. pp. 16. **H.S.P.**

Resolutions concerning Commerce.

163. Resolves of Congress / concerning / Trade. / Together with the Act for establishing a / Naval-Office / In the State of Massachusetts-Bay. / Also, / The Forms established by the General / Court to be used by the Naval-Officers in / said State. / Printed by Order of said Court / Boston: N. E. / Printed by J. Gill, M,DCC,LXXVII. 8°. pp. 28. **M.**

Journals.

164. Journals / of / Congress, / Containing / the / Proceedings / From January 1st, 1777, to January 1st, 1778. / Published by order of Congress. / Volume III. / Philadelphia. / Printed by John Dunlap. 8°. pp. 603. xxii.

As originally issued this volume contained 6 additional leaves, being the index to volume 1, but as these have generally been removed and placed in that volume, I have not included them in the above collation.

1778.

Feb. 3. Oath of Allegiance.

165. I / do acknowledge the United States of Ame-/rica to be Free, Independent and Sovereign States, ... / 16°. Broadside. **P.L.**

By an oversight, this title was given under Oct. 21, 1776, though it is the revised oath of allegiance adopted Feb. 3, 1778.

Feb. 3. Resolutions concerning Disaffected Persons.

166. In Congress, / February 3. 1778. F°. Broadside. **S., V.S.**

Feb. 6. Treaty with France. See No. 173.

Feb. 6. Resolutions on Hospitals.

167. Rules and directions / for the better regulating the Military Hospital of the United States : / In consequence of a Resolve of the Honourable the Continental Congress, the 6th of / February, 1778; to be punctually observed by the Officers, Nurses, &c. of the / Eastern Department. / . . . . . [signed] P. Turner, Surg. Gen. M. H. E. D. F°. Broadside.

Feb. 27. Resolutions concerning Loyalists.

168. The deluded tools of the enemy, who are committing treason against *America*, would / do well to peruse the following Resolution of Congress with attention. They may / rest as-

sured, those of them who shall be hardy enough to violate the act, will meet with / condign and exemplary punishment whenever they are taken. / February 27, 1778. F°. Broadside. M.

Mar. 2. Resolutions concerning Cavalry.

169. In Congress, / March 2, 1778.
F°. Broadside. S.

Apr. 6. Resolutions concerning Pulaski's Corps.

170. Congress having resolved to raise a Corps consisting of / Infantry and Cavalry, to be commanded by General / Count Pulaski, ... / . . . . .
4°. Broadside. V.S.

Apr. 23. Resolutions concerning Pardons.

171. In Congress, / April 23, 1778 / . . . . . / Yorktown: Printed by Hall and Sellers.
4°. Broadside. S.

" *Ordered*, That five hundred copies in English and two hundred in German be printed." — *Journal*.

May 2. Resolutions concerning Lottery.

172. In Congress, May 2, 1778.
8°. Broadside. V.S.

May 4. Treaty with France.

173. Treaties / of / Amity and Commerce, / and of / Alliance / Eventual and Defensive / between / His Most Christian Majesty / and the / Thirteen United States / of America. / Philadelphia: / Printed by John Dunlap. / MDCCLXXVIII.
4°. pp. (2) 10, (2) 11-34.

" *Ordered*, That three hundred copies of the Treaties of Amity and Commerce, and of Alliance . . . be printed." — *Journals*.

174. Treaties / of / Amity and Commerce, / and of / Alliance / Eventual and Defensive, / between / His Most Christian Majesty / and the / Thirteen United States / Of America. / Hartford: / Re-printed, and sold by Hudson and Goodwin. / MDCCLXXIX. 8°. pp. 32. P.L.

175. The Treaties between His Most Christian Majesty and the Thirteen United States of America. Philadelphia printed, London reprinted by J. Stockdale. MDCCLXXXII. 8°. pp. 40.

176. The / Treaties of Amity / and / Commerce, / and of / Alliance, / Eventual and Defensive, / between His Most Christian Majesty / and the / Thirteen United States / of / North America. / Norwich: / Printed by John Trumbull, at the / Printing Office near the Meeting-House. / M.DCC.LXXIX. / 8°. pp. 24. M.

177. + Newbern, N. C. Printed by John Davis. 1778.

Title from Weeke's *Printing in North Carolina*.

180. The / Articles / Published by Congress, / of a / Treaty of Amity and Commerce, / and of a / Treaty of Alliance / Between the Crown of France / And these United States, / Duly entered into and executed at Paris, on / the 6th day of February last, by a Minister / properly authorized by His Most / Christian Majesty on the one part, and the Commissi-/oners of Congress on the other part. / Also the / Articles / of / Confederation and Perpetual / Union / Between the United States of America, as pro-/posed by Congress to the Legislatures of the / different states. / Lancaster: Printed by John Dunlap.
Sm. 12°. pp. (2) 2-12, (17).

May 9. Address to the Inhabitants.

181. Address of the Congress / to the / Inhabitants of the United States of America. / Lancaster, printed by John Dunlap.
F°. Broadside.

Drafted by R. H. Lee, Samuel Chase and Governeur Morris. It was adopted May 8th.

In Lee's *Life of R. H. Lee* it is claimed that it is from his pen, but on the contrary Sparks in his *Life of G. Morris* states that the rough draft is among the Morris papers, in Morris's handwriting.

May 9. Address to the Inhabitants.

182. An / Address of the Congress / to the / Inhabitants of the United States of America. / York-Town: Printed by Hall and Sellers.
F°. Broadside.

May 9. Proclamation concerning Privateers.

183. A Proclamation. / Lancaster, Printed by John Dunlap. F°. Broadside. S.

184. A Proclamation. / . . . . . / Given in Congress at York, in the State of Pennsylvania, this Ninth / Day of May, Anno Domini One Thousand Seven Hundred and Seventy-Eight. / Henry Laurens, President. / . . . / Yorktown: Printed by John Dunlap. F°. Broadside. V.S.

May 27. New Regulations for Army.

185. In Congress, / 27th May, 1778 / Establishment of the / American Army. / York-Town: Printed by John Dunlap. F°. 1 l.

See, also, under Nov. 21, 1778.

June 3. Prize Numbers in Lottery.

186. A List / of the / Fortunate Numbers / in the / First Class / of the / United States Lottery. / . . . . . / Printed by Hall and Sellers.
8°. pp. 55.

Aug. 14. Resolutions on supplying Enemy with Food.

187. In Congress, / August 14, 1778 / . . . . . / Printed by Hall and Sellers. 1779.
4°. Broadside.

Aug. 21. Court Martial of Charles Lee.

188. Proceedings / of a / General Court Marshall, / Held at Brunswick, / In the State of New-Jersey, / by order of / His Excellency / General Washington, / Commander in Chief / Of the Army of / The United States of America, / For the Trial of / Major General Lee. / July 4th, 1778. / Major General Lord Stirling, President. / Philadelphia: / Printed by John Dunlap, in Market-Street / MDCCLXXVIII.
F°. pp. 62.

" *Ordered*, That one hundred copies of the proceedings of the court martial on the trial of major general Lee, be printed for the use of the members." — *Journal*.

Reprinted in 1823 and 1864.

Sept. 19. Report on Treasury and Finance.

189. Your Committee, to whom it was referred to consider and report on the Currency / and Finance of these United States, beg leave to report, / . . . . . F°. Broadside. S.D.

" *Resolved*, That a committee of five be appointed to consider the state of the money and finances of the United States and to report thereon . . .

" The members chosen Mr. R. Morris, Mr. Gerry, Mr. R. H. Lee, Mr. Witherspoon and Mr. G. Morris . . .

" *Resolved*, That sixty copies, of said report be printed for the use of the members, and that the printer be under oath not to divulge any part of the said report, nor to strike more than sixty copies, and to deliver to the secretary of Congress said copies, together with the proofs and unfinished sheets." — *Journal*.

Oct. 8. Court Martial on St. Clair.

190. Proceedings / of a / General Court Martial, / Held at White Plains, / In the State of / New-York. / By Order of his Excellency / General Washington, / Commander in Chief / Of the Army of / The United States of America, / For the Trial of / Major General St. Clair, / August 25, 1778. / Major General Lincoln, President. / Philadelphia: / Printed by Hall and Sellers, in Market-Street. / MDCCLXXVIII. Fº. pp. 52. Map.

" *Ordered*, That one hundred copies of the proceedings of the court-martial on the trial of major general St. Clair, together with his defence, be printed for the use of the members." — *Journal.*

Oct. 8. Resolutions against Limitation.

191. In Congress, / October 8, 1778. / . . . . / Philadelphia: Printed by John Dunlap. / Fº. Broadside. V.S.

See also No. 204.

Oct. 30. Manifesto on Conduct of War.

192. By the Congress of the United States / of America. / A Manifesto. Fº. Broadside.

Nov. 17. Proclamation of Thanksgiving.

193. A Proclamation / . . . . . / Done in Congress, this 17th Day of November, 1778 . . . / . . . . . / Henry Laurens. Fº. Broadside.
Prepared by the Chaplains of the Congress.

Nov. 24. Resolutions on Continental Army.

194. In Congress / November 24, 1778. Fº. Broadside. M.
Settling the rank of officers.

195. In Congress, May 27, 1778. / Establishment of the American Army. Fº. Broadside. V.S.
Contains the additional resolves of May 29, and Nov. 24, 1778.

Dec. 3. Court Martial of Schuyler.

196. Proceedings / of a / General Court Martial, / Held at Major General Lincoln's Quarters, / Near Quaker-Hill, / In the State of / New-York, / By Order of his Excellency / General Washington, / Commander in Chief / Of the Army of / The United States of America, / For the Trial of / Major General Schuyler, / October 1, 1778. / Major General Lincoln, President. / Philadelphia: / Printed by Hall and Sellers, in Market-street. / MDCCLXXVIII. Fº. pp. 62.
Reprinted in *Collections of the N. Y. Historical Society for 1879.*

Health of Soldiers.

197. Directions / For Preserving / The Health of / Soldiers: / recommended to / The Consideration of the / Officers / Of the Army of the / United / States. / By Benjamin Rush, M. D. / Published by Order of the Board / Of War / Lancaster: Printed by John Dunlap, / In Queen-Street. / M.DCC.LXXVIII. 12º. pp. 8.
Reprinted in 1865 and 1871.

Journal.

198. Journal / of / Congress, / Containing / the / Proceedings / From January 1st, 1778, to January 1st, 1779. / Published by order of Congress. / Volume IV. / Philadelphia: / Printed by David C. Claypoole, / Printer to the Honorable the Congress. 8º. pp. (2), 748, lxxxix, (4).

1779.

Jan. 2. Description of Counterfeits.

199. Description/of/Counterfeit Bills, / Which were done in Imitation of the True Ones ordered by the Honorable / the Continental Congress, / Bearing Date 20th May, 1777, and 11th April, 1778. Fº. Broadside.

Jan. 9. Resolutions on Prisoners.

200. In Congress, / January 9, 1779. / . . . . . / Philadelphia, Printed by John Dunlap. Fº. Broadside.

Jan. 12. Circular Letter of Instructions.

201. Treasury-Office, January 12, 1779. Fº. Broadside. P.L.
A letter to the Commissioners of the loan office on exchanging the counterfeited emissions,

Jan. 12. Directions for retiring Currency.

202. Instructions / from the / Board of Treasury / to the respective / Commissioners of the Continental / Loan-Offices. / Treasury-Office, January 12, 1779. Fº. Broadside. P.L.

Jan. 14. Address to the People on the Currency.

203. In Congress, January 13, 1779./ . . . . . / Philadelphia, Printed by John Dunlap. Fº. 1 l. P.L.

With the resolutions adopted Jan. 2, and Jan. 5, and the address adopted Jan. 13, 1779. The portions adopted Jan. 2 and 5 were reported by the board of treasury. That of Jan. 13, by a committee.
The committee on the treasury, who were directed to extract from the journals the several resolutions respecting finance, in order that they may be printed reported that they had executed that business, and are of the opinion that the circular letter and the resolutions of the 2d and 5th instant be printed on one sheet . . . [and] that one hundred copies . . . be struck off. . . . *Resolved*, That Congress agree to the report. — *Journal.*

Jan. 14. Resolutions on Currency.

204. In Congress, / October 8, 1778. / . . . . . / Philadelphia. Printed by John Dunlap. Fº. Broadside. P.L.

With the additional resolves of Nov. 19, 1778, Jan. 1, and Jan. 14, 1779. Only 100 copies printed.

Feb. 1. Journals. See No. 233.

Feb. 23. Orders to Commissioners of Loan Offices.

205. Treasury-Office, / February 23d, 1779. Fº. Broadside. P.L.

Mar. 2. Resolutions on Arrearages.

206. In Congress, / March 2, 1779 / . . . . . / Printed by Hall and Sellers. 1779. Fº. Broadside. D.S.

Mar. 5. Resolutions on Soldiers' Certificates.

207. In Congress, March 5, 1779. / . . . . . / Printed by Hall and Sellers. 1779. / Fº. Broadside. D.S.

Mar. 6. Resolutions concerning Admiralty Decisions.

208. In Congress, / March 6, 1779. / . . . . . / Philadelphia, Printed by David C. Claypoole, Printer to / the Honorable the Congress of the United States of America. / Fº. Broadside. V.S.

Mar. 20. Recommendation of Fast.

209. Proclamation. / Philadelphia: Printed by Hall and Sellers. Fº. Broadside. V.S.
Drafted by G. Morris, Drayton and Paca.

Mar. 23. Ordinance for Clothing Dep.

210. In Congress, / March 23, 1779. / Ordinance for regulating the Clothing Department for the Armies of the United States. /
          Fº. Broadside. V.S.

Prepared by Duane, Root, M. Smith, G. Morris and Laurens, after consultation with Washington.

211. In Congress, / March 23, 1779. / Ordinance for regulating the Clothing Department for / the Armies of the United States. / . . . . . / Printed by Hall and Sellers.   Fº. 1 l. D.S.

Mar. 29. Steuben's Regulations.

212. Regulations / for the / Order and Discipline / of the / Troops / of the / United States. / Part I. / Philadelphia : / Printed by Styner and Cist, in Second-street. / MDCCLXXIX.
          12º. pp. 154, (9), 8 plates.

" A letter of the 25th from baron Steuben was read, accompanied with a system of regulations for the infantry of the United States ; also a letter from the board of war, representing that baron Steuben, inspector general, has formed a system of exercise and discipline for the infantry of the United States : that the same has been submitted to the inspection of the commander in chief, and his remarks thereon and amendments incorporated in the work : that it has been examined with attention by the board, and is highly approved, as being calculated to produce important advantages to the states ; and therefore praying ' that it may receive the sanction of Congress and be committed to the press :' whereupon, . . .
" Ordered, That the board of war cause as many copies thereof to be printed as they shall deem requisite for the use of the troops." — Journal.

213. Regulations for the Order and Discipline of the Troops of the United States. Part I. Hartford : Hudson and Goodwin. [1779].
          Sm. 8º. pp. 138, (6), plates.

Title from Steven's Historical Collections, I., 88.

213ª. + Hartford. N. Patten. [1780.]

214. Regulations / for the / Order and Discipline / of the / Troops / of the / United States / Part I. / Hartford : / Printed by Hudson & Goodwin. [1782.] 12º. pp. 89, (6), 8 plates. P.L.

For other editions see under 1785.

214*. Regulations / for the / Order and Discipline / of the / Troops / of the / United States. / Part 1. / Philadelphia : / Printed by Charles Cist, at the corner of / Fourth and Arch-streets. M,DCC,LXXXV.   8º. pp. (4), 151 (7).

Apr. 5. Directions for Transmitting Currency.

215. Treasury-Office. April 5th, 1779.
          Fº. Broadside. P.L.

Apr. 22. Treasury Reports.

216. Reports / of the / Board of Treasury / relative to finance /   Fº. 7 ll. L.C.P.

See Journal for Apr. 22, 1779.

May 10. Report on Exchange of Prisoners.

217. Report / of / Commissioners / for / Settling a Cartel / for the / Exchange of Prisoners. / Philadelphia : / Printed by David C. Claypoole / Printer to the Honorable the Congress of / the United States of America. / MDCCLXXIX.
          8º. pp. 20.

Ordered, That the report of Colonel Davies and Harrison to the Commander in Chief, of their conference aforesaid be published. — Journal.

May 26. Address to the States.

218. To the / Inhabitants / of the / United States of America / Philadelphia : Printed by David C. Claypoole, Printer to the / Honorable the Congress of the United States of America.
          Fº. 1 l.

Dickinson, Drayton and Duane were appointed to prepare this. It was written by Dickinson, and is republished in his Writings, 11.

219. Address of the Continental Congress to the people of the United States, with the endorsement of the Massachusetts Bay Province.
          Fº. Broadside.

Title from the F. S. Drake auction sale catalogue, lot 716.

220. To the / Inhabitants / of the / United States of America. / [Hartford, 1779.]
          Fº. Broadside. P.L.

With the order of Jonathan Trumbull.

221. Circular Letter from Congress to sustain the credit of the United States. Poughkeepsie. 1779.

Title from auction catalogue.

July 23. Report on Departments.

222. [Report of a committee appointed for enquiring into and regulating and retrenching the expenses of the respective boards and departments.]   º. pp.

" The committee [of Dickinson, Sherman and Scudder] brought in a report.
" Ordered, That sixty copies be printed for the use of the members." — Journal.

July 30. Treasury Ordinance.

223. In Congress, July 30, 1779. / Ordinance for establishing a Board of Treasury, and the proper / Officers for managing the finances of these United States.   Fº. Broadside. D.S.

Sept. 13. Circular Letter.

224. A / Circular Letter / from the / Congress / of the / United States of America / to their / Constituents. / Philadelphia : / Printed by David C. Claypoole, / Printer to the Honorable the Congress.   8º. pp. 12. H.S.P.

On Aug. 10, it was " resolved that a committee of three be appointed to prepare a circular letter to the several states," but contrary to custom, no members were named, and it is evident that while the Congress agreed to the letter they could not agree to the men who were to prepare it. It was to deal partly with the French alliance and the consequent letters of the French Minister, and the Franklin-Deane-Lee imbroglio had rent the Congress into factions, each of which feared some partizan attempt to influence the people through this official letter. Finally after nearly a month's dead-lock the Congress on Sept. 8 requested their president, John Jay, to prepare a letter, which he reported Sept. 13, and which was unanimously accepted. It is the only case in the history of the while Continental Congress of one man being named to prepare a paper.

225. A / Circular Letter / from the / Congress / of the / United States of America / to their / Constituents. / Philadelphia : Printed september, 1779 / Boston : Reprinted by Order of the / General Assembly of the State of Massachusetts Bay.   8º. pp. 15. P.L.

226. A / Circular Letter / from the / Congress / of the / United States of America / to their / Constituents. / Philadelphia, Printed : / New London : Re-printed by T. Green. 12º. pp. 19.

Nov. 25. Resolutions for Supplies.

227. In Congress, / November 25th, 1779. / ..... / Philadelphia : Printed by David C. Claypoole, Printer to the Honorable the Congress. Fº. Broadside. **D.S.**

Enumerating the articles to be delivered to each officer for the year.

Dec. 3. Table of Loan Office Certificates.

228. Table / Of the Sums actually in circulation / between the 1st of September and the / 30th of November, 1779, inclusive, / and of the Sums that will be in circu- / lation from thence to the 28th of Fe- / bruary, 1780, to serve as a rule to / the Commissaries of the several Loan- / Offices of the United States in the / payment of interest due, and that will / become due, on Loan-Office Certifi- / cates. / [Colophon] Philadelphia : Printed by David C. Claypoole. Sº. pp. 7. **N.J.H.S.**

Signed Robert Troup, Secretary. December 3d, 1779.

Prize Numbers in Lottery.

229. A / List / of the / Fortunate Numbers / in the / Second Class / of the / United States Lottery. / Philadelphia : / Printed by John Dunlap, in Market-street / MDCCLXXIX. / Sº. pp. 54. **H.S.P.**

Table of Interest.

230. A / Table / of the / First Years Interest / To be paid on the Monies which have / been placed in the several Continental / Loan Offices, between the 1st of June / and 1st of December 1778, calculated / for each day on which the Money may / have been deposited in Pursuance of a Re- / solution of the Congress of the 29th of / June 1779 : / ..... [signed] R. Troup. Sº. pp. 7. **N.J.H.S.**

This was reported by the board of treasury Aug. 6, 1779, but was recommitted by order of Congress on Aug. 16. I do not find when it was adopted.

Observations on the Revolution.

231. Observations / on the / American Revolution. / Published / according to a resolution / of Congress, / by their committee. / For the / Consideration of those who are desirous / of comparing / The Conduct of the opposed Parties, / and / The several Consequences which have / flowed from it. / Philadelphia : / Printed by Styner and Cist, in Second-Street. / M DCC LXXIX. Sº. pp. (4), 122.

On Oct. 26, 1778, G. Morris, W. H. Drayton and R. H. Lee were appointed a committee " to superintend the publication of such matters relating to the disputes, petitions and negotiations to and with the court of Great-Britain, and such notes and explanations thereon as to them shall appear proper; and that they agree with the printer for thirteen hundred copies of such publication, on account of Congress." On Nov. 13, S. Adams was added to this committee, and they were " impowered to proceed in the publication as they judge proper." These two references are the only ones in the Journal I have been able to find; but the work was not published till early in Mar., 1779.

It is severely attacked by Common Sense (Thomas Paine) in the *Pennsylvania Packet* for Mar. 20, 1779, and he says. it was written by Drayton and Morris, the latter performing the greater part. In Spark's *Life of Morris* it is said to be entirely written by him. It is, however, largely a compilation.

232. ✝ Providence. Re-printed by John Carter 1780. Sº. pp. 126.

Was also reprinted in Almon's *Remembrancer* for 1780.

Journals. January.

233. Journals / of / Congress / from Friday, January 1st, / to / Monday, February 1st, 1779. Philadelphia : / Printed by David C. Claypoole, Printer to / the Congress of the United States of America. / MDCCLXXIX. Fº. pp. 12.

On Mar. 31, 1779, Congress " *resolved*, that from the first of January last the Journal of this house . . . be printed immediately ; and that for the future [it] . . . be printed weekly." In pursuance of this, three monthly parts, for the past months of January, February and March were printed, and after that it was continued each week in weekly parts.

It is needless to say that these monthly and weekly issues are of the greatest rarity, and are, moreover, of value, as they include much matter not printed in the ordinary yearly volume. The only perfect copies I know of are in the Historical Society of Pennsylvania and the library of Gordon L. Ford, of Brooklyn, N. Y. There are a few old parts in the N. Y. State and Connecticut State libraries. See *Proceedings of the Massachusetts Historical Society.*

Journals. February.

234. Journals / of / Congress, / from / Monday, February 1st, / to / Monday, March 1st, 1779. / Philadelphia : / Printed by David C. Claypoole, / Printer to the Honorable the Congress of / the United States of America. 8º. pp. 50.

Journals. March.

235. Journals / of / Congress / from / Monday, March 1st, / to / Tuesday, March 30, 1779, inclusive. / Philadelphia : / Printed by David C. Claypoole, / Printer to the Honorable the Congress of / the United States of America. 8º. pp. 56.

Journals. Weekly issue.

236. Journals / of / Congress, / from / Wednesday, March thirty-first, / to / Saturday, April tenth, 1779, inclusive. / Philadelphia : / Printed by David C. Claypoole, / Printer to the hon. the Congress of / the United States of America. 8º. pp. 24.

The first of the weekly parts. The titles of the following successive issues vary from this only as noted.

237. * / Monday, April 12th, / to / Saturday, April 17th, 1779. / inclusive. / 8º. pp. 19.

238. * / Monday, April 19th, / to / Saturday, April 24th, 1779. / inclusive. / 8º. pp. 24.

239. * / Saturday, April 24th, / to / Monday, May 3d, 1779. / 8º. pp. 16.

240. * / Saturday, May 1st, / to / Monday, May 10th, 1779. / 8º. pp. 15.

241. * / Monday, May 10th, / to / Saturday, May 15th, 1779, / inclusive. / 8º. pp. 15.

242. * / Monday, May 17th, / to / Saturday, May 22d, 1779, / inclusive. / 8º. pp. 15.

243. * / Monday, May 24th, / to / Saturday, May 29th, 1779, / inclusive. / 8º. pp. 20.

244. * / Monday, May 31st, / to / Saturday, June 5th, 1779, / inclusive. / 8º. pp. 15.

245. * / Monday, June 7th. / to / Saturday, June 12th, 1779, / inclusive. / 8º. pp. 19.

246. * / Monday, June 14th, / to / Saturday, June 19th, 1779, / inclusive. / 8º. pp. 10.

247. * / Monday, June 21st, / to / Saturday, June 26th, 1779, / inclusive. / 8º. pp. 13.

248. * / Monday, June 28th, / to / Saturday, July 3d, 1779, / inclusive. / 8º. pp. 15.

249. * / Monday, July 5th, / to / Saturday, July 12th [*sic*], 1779, / inclusive. / 8º. pp. 7.

PUBLICATIONS OF THE CONTINENTAL CONGRESS.

250. * / Monday, July 12th, / to / Saturday, July 17th, 1779. / inclusive. / 8°. pp. 10.

251. * / Monday, July 19th, / to / Saturday, July 24th, 1779, / inclusive. / 8°. pp. 14.

252. * / Monday, July 26th, / to / Saturday, July 31st, 1779. / inclusive. / 8°. pp. 16.

With this issue the imprint was changed to "Philadelphia: / Printed by David C. Claypoole, / Printer to the Honourable Congress," and so remained for the rest of the series.

253. * / Monday, August 2d, / to / Saturday, August 7th, 1779, / inclusive. / 8°. pp. 11.

254. * / Monday, August 9th, / to / Saturday, August 14th, 1779, / inclusive. / 8°. pp. 10.

255. * / Monday, August 16th, / to / Saturday 21st, 1779, / inclusive. / 8°. pp. 13.

256. * / Monday, August 23d, / to / Saturday, August 28th, 1779, / inclusive. / 8°. pp. 14.

257. * / Monday, August 30th, / to / Saturday, September 4th, 1779, / inclusive. / 8°. pp. 12.

258. * / Monday, September 6th, / to / Saturday, September 11th, 1779, / inclusive. / 8°. pp. 10.

259. * / Monday, September 13th, / to / Saturday, September 18th, 1779, / inclusive. / 8°. pp. 22.

260. * / Monday, September 20th, / to / Saturday, September 25th, 1779, / inclusive. / 8°. pp. 9.

261. * / Sunday, September 26th, / to / Saturday, October 2d, 1779, / inclusive. 8°. pp. 11.

262. * / Monday, October 4th, / to / Saturday, October 9th, 1779, / inclusive. / 8°. pp. 11.

263. * / Monday, October 11th, / to / Saturday, October 16th, 1779, / inclusive. / 8°. pp. 8.

264. * / Monday, October 18th, / to / Saturday, October 23d, 1779, / inclusive. / 8°. pp. 12.

265. * / Monday, October 25th, / to / Saturday, October 30th, 1779. / inclusive. / 8°. pp. 13.

266. * / Monday, November 1st, / to / Saturday, November 6th, 1779, / inclusive. / 8°. pp. 7.

267. * / Monday, November 8th, / to / Saturday, November 12th, 1779, / inclusive. / 8°. pp. 11.

268. * / Monday, November 15th, / to / Saturday, November 20th, 1779, / inclusive. / 8°. pp. (19.)

269. * / Monday, November 22d, / to / Saturday, November 27th, 1779, / inclusive. / 8°. pp. 25.

270. * / Monday, November 29th, / to / Saturday, December 4th, 1779, / inclusive. / 8°. pp. 12.

271. * / Monday, December 6th, / to / Saturday, December 11th, 1779, / inclusive. / 8°. pp. 10.

272. * / Monday, December 13th, / to / Saturday, December 18th, 1779, / inclusive. / 8°. pp. 12.

273. * / Monday, December 20th, / to / Friday, December 31st, 1779, / inclusive. / 8°. pp. 16.

Journal.

274. Journals / of / Congress. / Containing / the / Proceedings / From January 1, 1779, to January 1, 1780. / Published by Order of Congress. / Volume V. / Philadelphia: / Printed by David C. Claypoole. / M,DCC,LXXXII.
8°. pp. 464, (15), lxxiv.

In the first issue of this volume pages 25 and 28, and 29 and 32, backed each other and were duplicated. There were no pages 26, 27, 30 and 31. These errors are corrected in most copies.

1780.

Feb. 25. Resolution on State Quotas.

275. In Congress, February 25, 1780. 4°. pp. 4. P.L.

A resolution fixing the quotas of supplies from the states for the ensuing campaign.

May 2. Instruction for Privateers.

276. In Congress, / May 2, 1780. / Instructions / to the / Captains and Commanders / Of Private Armed Vessels, / Which shall have Commissions, or Letters of / Marque and Reprisal.
F°. 1 l. S.D.

July 15. Plan of Quarter Master's Dep't.

277. Plan / for Conducting / The Quartermaster General's Department, / Agreed to In Congress, / July 15th, 1780. / Philadelphia: / Printed by David C. Claypoole, / Printer to the Honourable the Congress. / M,DCC,LXXX.
8°. pp. 16. L.C.P., S.D.

Aug. 26. Resolutions on the Currency.

278. Extract from the Journal of Congress. / August 26, 1780. / F°. 1 l.

Sept. 1. Proclamation.

279. By the United States in Congress / Assembled, / A Proclamation. / ..... / Done in Congress, this First Day of September, in the Year of our Lord One / Thousand Seven Hundred and Eighty. F°. Broadside.

Sept. 25. Plan of Inspecting Dep't.

280. Plan / For / Conducting / the / Inspector's Department of the / United States. / Philadelphia: / Printed by David C. Claypoole, / Printer to the Honourable the Congress.
8°. pp. 8. L.C.P.

Sept. 30. Plan of Hospital Dep't.

281. Plan / for / Conducting / the / Hospital Department of the / United States. /Philadelphia: / Printed by David C. Claypoole, / Printer to the Honourable the Congress. 8°. pp. 8.

Oct. 30. Resolutions on Southern Army.

282. In Congress. / October 30, 1780. / ..... / Philadelphia, Printed by David C. Claypoole, Printer to the Honourable the Congress.
F°. Broadside. P.L.

Prize Numbers in Lottery.

283. A / List / of the / Fortunate Numbers / in the Third Class / of the / United States Lottery. / Philadelphia: / Printed by Hall and Sellers, at the / New Printing-Office, opposite the Jersey Market. / M.DCC LXXX. /
8°. Title, 1 l. pp. 57. P.H.S.

18

Table of Interest.

284. Table / for the / Payment / of the / Second Years Interest / due on / All Sums loaned to the United States / between The 28th of February, 1778, / and / The 28th of February 1780. / Philadelphia : / Printed by David C. Claypoole, Printer to the Honorable the Congress.   S⁰.   pp. 18.   **N.J.H.S.**

Table of Loan Office Certificates.

285. Table / for / The Payment / of / Principal and Interest of / Loans, / agreeable to / The Resolutions / of / Congress, / of / The twenty-eighth day of June, / 1780. / Philadelphia : / Printed by David C. Claypoole, / Printer to the Honourable the Congress. / M,DCC,LXXX.   S⁰.   pp. 23.   **P.H.S.**

Reprinted in Phillips's *Sketches*, II, 310.

286. Tables / for / The Payment / of / Principle [sic] and Interest / of / Loans, / agreeable to / The Resolutions / of / Congress / of / The twenty-eighth day of June, / 1780. / Philadelphia : / Printed and Sold by T. Bradford / in Front Street, the fourth door from / the Coffee-House. 1783.   18mo. pp. 36.

Court Martial on Arnold.

287. Proceedings / of a / General Court Martial / of the Line, / Held at Raritan, / in the State of / New Jersey, / By Order of his Excellency / George Washington, Esq. / General and Commander in Chief / Of the Army of the / United States of America, / For the Trial of / Major General Arnold / June 1, 1779. / Major General Howe, President. / Published by Order of Congress. / Philadelphia : / Printed by Francis Bailey, in Market-Street. / M.DCC.LXXX.   F⁰.   pp. 55.   **P.N.S.**

" Feb. 15, 1780 . . . *Resolved*, That fifty copies of the trial of major general Arnold be printed at the public expence." — *Journals.*

288. Proceedings / of a / General Court Martial / for the Trial of / Major General Arnold. / With an / Introduction, Notes, and Index. / New York : / Privately Printed, / 1865.   S⁰.   pp. xxix, (2) 182, portrait.

135 copies reprinted.

Trial of André.

289. Proceedings / of a / Board / of / General Officers, / Held by Order of / His Excellency Gen. Washington, / Commander in Chief of the Army of the United States / of America. / Respecting / Major John André, / Adjutant General of the British Army / September 29, 1780 / Philadelphia : / Printed by Francis Bailey, / in Market-Street. / M.DCC.LXXX. S⁰.   pp. (2) 21.   **N.**

290. Proceedings / of a / Board / of / General Officers, / Held by Order of / His Excellency Gen. Washington, / Commander in Chief of the Army of the United / States of America. / Respecting / Major John Andre, / Adjutant General of the British Army. / September 29, 1780. / To which are Appended, The several Letters which / passed to and from New-York on the Occasion, &c. / Philadelphia, printed / Hartford : / Re-printed by B. Webster. / M,DCC,LXXX.   Sm. S⁰.   pp. (2) 32.   **M.H.S.**

291. Proceedings of a / Board of General Officers, / Held by Order of / His Excellency

Gen. Washington, / Commander in Chief of the Army of the United States of America, / Respecting / Major John André, / Adjutant General of the British Army. / September 29, 1780. / To which are appended, / The several Letters which passed to and from New-York on the Occasion. / Published by Order of Congress. / Providence, / Printed and Sold by John Carter.   S⁰.   pp. 16.   **J.C.B.**

292. Proceedings / of a / Board / of / General Officers, / held by order of / His Excellency General Washington, / Commander in Chief of the Army of the United States of America. / Respecting / Major John Andre, / Adjutant General of the British Army. / September 29, 1780. / Philadelphia Printed — New-York Re-printed / By James Rivington, opposite the Coffee-House Bridge.   4⁰.   pp. 13.   **N.**

293. Minutes / of a / Court of Inquiry, / upon the case of / Major John André, / with / accompanying documents, / published in 1780 by order of Congress. / With / An Additional Appendix / containing copies of the papers found upon / Major Andre when arrested, and other / documents relating to the subject. / Albany : / J. Munsell, 78 State Street. / 1865.   Sm. 4⁰.   pp. iv, 66, portrait.

100 copies printed, with an introduction by F. B. Hough.

294. Proceedings / of a / Board of General Officers / respecting / Major John André / New York / Privately Printed / 1867. /   S⁰.   pp. (6), 21.

40 copies printed by F. S. Hoffman in " literal facsimile of the original edition, as nearly as modern old style will permit."

Journals.

295. Journals / of / Congress, / from / January 1st, 1780, / to / January 1st, 1781. / Published by Order of Congress. / Philadelphia : / Printed by David C. Claypoole, / Printer to the Honorable the Congress.   S⁰.   **P.L., H.S.P.**

This edition of the Journal was issued in monthly parts, in continuation of Nos. 233-274. Like those, it contains much matter omitted in later editions. The captions and collation of the parts are as follows : —

Journals of Congress, | For January, 1780. | pp. 38, 2 blank pp.
Journals of Congress, | For February, 1780. | pp. (41)-73. 1 blank p.
Journals of Congress, | For March, 1780. | pp. (75)-106.
Journals of Congress, | For April, 1780. | pp. (106)-131.
Journals of Congress, | For May, 1780. | pp. (132)-162, 1 blank p.
Journals of Congress, | For June, 1780. | pp. (164)-198, 1 blank p.
Journals of Congress, | For July, 1780. | pp. (199)-237, 1 blank p.
Journals of Congress, | For August, 1780. | pp. (239)-274.
Journals of Congress, | For September, 1780. | pp. (275)-314.
Journals of Congress, | For October, 1780. | pp. (315)-349, 1 blank p.
Journals of Congress, | For November, 1780. | pp. (351)-384, 2 blank pp.
Journals of Congress, | For December, 1780. | pp. (385)-403, 3 blank pp.
General Index | To Volume VI* | pp. (i)-xxxviii.
Appendix. | Expenditures. | pp. (3).

" N. B. The numbers 106, 302, 303 are each found twice at the head of a page." — *Journals.*

296. Resolutions, / Acts and Orders / of / Congress, / For the Year 1780. / Volume VI. / Published by Order of Congress. / Printed by John Dunlap.   S⁰.   pp. 257, xliii.

This is only an abridgment of No. 295, but is usually bound with sets of the Journal, as the volume for 1780. It was probably printed in 1787, in pursuance of the resolution of September 13, 1786.

1781.

Feb. 3. Resolution on Impost.

297. Resolved, That it be recommended to the several / states, as indispensably necessary to the restoration of public credit, ... / ... to vest in the united / states in congress assembled. a power to levy for the / use of the united states, a duty of five per cent ad / valorem.   F°. Broadside.

Mar. 3. Report on Convention Prisoners.

298. United States in Congress assembled, / March 3, 1781.   F°. 1 l. S.D.
.Report of Kean, Gorham, Pinckney, Smith and Grayson.

May 26. Plan of Bank of North America.

299. Plan for Establishing a National Bank for the United States .... To which is annexed, a Resolution of Congress, of the 26th of May 1781, acceding thereto; And a Particular Explanation of the Use of said Bank, By Robert Morris, Esquire, Superintendant [sic] of the Finance of America. Providence: .... Bennet. Wheeler [1781.]   8°. pp. 111
Title from Sabin. Cf. Journals May 26 and Dec. 31 1781.

Dec. 4. Ordinance for Marine Captures.

300. An Ordinance, / Ascertaining what Captures on / Water shall be lawful. / In pursuance of the Powers delegated by the Confederation in Cases of / Capture on Water: / ..... / Philadelphia: Printed by David C. Claypoole, in Market-Street. /   F°. Broadside. V.S., S.
See Jan. 8, 1782, infra.

Prize Numbers in Lottery.

301. A List / Of the Fortunate Numbers / In the Fourth Class / of the / United States Lottery. / [Colophon.] Printed by Hall and Sellers. [1781.] /   Sm. 4°. pp. 83 (1). H.S.P.
Drawn on April 2, 1781, In pursuance of a resolution of Congress adopted Feb. 6, 1781.

Rules for Troops.

302. Rules and Articles for the Better Government of the Troops of the United States. Philadelphia. MDCCLXXXI.   8°. pp. 36.
Title from Sabin.

303. The / Constitutions / of the / Several Independent States / of / America; / the / Declaration of Independence; / the / Articles of Confederation / between the said States; / the / Treaties between His Most Christian Majesty / and the United States of America. / Published by order of Congress. / Philadelphia: / Printed by Francis Bailey, in Market Street. / M.DCC.LXXXI. /
          Sm. 8°. pp. (2) 3-226. P.H.S.
Printed in pursuance of a resolve of Dec. 29, 1780.

304.* Philadelphia printed; London reprinted, with an Advertisement By the Editor, For J. Stockdale, in Piccadilly; and sold by J. Walker. MDCCLXXXII.   8°. pp. viii, 168.
Title from Sabin.

305. The Constitution of the several Independent States of America; The Declaration of Independence; The Articles of Confederation between the said States; The Treaties between His Most Christian Majesty and the United States of America. With an Appendix, containing An Authentic Copy of the Treaty concluded between their High Mightinesses the States-General and the United States of America, and the Provisional Treaty. Published by order of Congress. Philadelphia Printed: London, Reprinted, with an Advertisement by J. L. De Lolme, J. Walker, J. Debrett. MDCCLXXXIII. 8°. pp. viii, 189, (2), portrait and map. J.C.B.

306. The / constitutions / of the several / independent states / of / America; / the Declaration of Independence; / and the / Articles of Confederation / between the said states. / To which are now added the / Declaration of rights; / the / Non-importation agreement; /. and the / Petition of Congress to the King; / delivered by Mr. Penn. / With an / appendix, / containing the / treaties between his most christian [sic] ma- / jesty and the United States of America; / and (never before published) / an authentic copy of the treaty con- / cluded between their high mightines- / ses the States-General, and the United / States of America. / The whole arranged, with a / preface and dedication, / By the Rev. William Jackson. / London: / Printed for J. Stockdale, in Piccadilly. 1783.   8°. (4) xxix, (2). 472, (4), portrait. B.

307. A Collection of the Constitutions of the Thirteen United States of North America ..... Published by Order of Congress. Philadelphia, Printed. Glasgow: Re-printed By John Bryce. M,DCC,LXXXIII. /   16°. pp. (2), 257.

308. Constitutions of the several Independent States of America. Dublin, 1783.

309. Constitutions / des / Treize États-Unis / de l'Amérique. / A Philadelphie; / et se trouve à Paris. /

Chez. { Ph.-D. Pierres, Imprimeur Ordinaire du Roi, / rue Saint-Jacques. / Pissot, père & fils, Libraires, quai des / Augustins. /
/ 1783.   8°. pp. (4), 540. B., L.B.
There are copies on large paper in 4°.
In Sabin's Dictionary another edition is given, but I think it is the same as this, since the contents are identical. It is said to have been translated by the Duc de Rochefoucauld.
Some copies seen have a supplementary 4 pages, being "Acte de la République de Virginia, / qui établit la liberté de Religion."

310. The / Constitutions / of the / several independent states / of America; / the / Declaration of Independence; / the / Articles of Confederation / between the said states; / the / Treaties between His Most Christian / Majesty and the United States of America. / — And the Treaties between their High / Mightinesses the States General of the / United Netherlands and the United States / of America. / Published originally by Order of Congress. / The Second edition / Boston: Printed by Norman and Brown, in / Marshall's-Lane, near the Boston-stone / M.DCC.LXXXV.
          12°. pp. 28, 5-180 (1), 1-29. B.
This includes the Definitive Treaty with England.

311. Constitutions of the several Independent States of America. New York: 1786. 18°. C.
Title from the Catalogue of 1864 of the Library of Congress.
Many editions succeed this, but only after the adoption of the Federal Constitution, as well as the alteration of several of the state constitutions, so as to essentially alter the contents of the collection. These have therefore been omitted.

Journals for 1781.

See nos. 321-2.

1782.

Jan. 8. Ordinance for Marine Captures.

312. An Ordinance / For Amending the Ordinance, ascertaining what Captures on Water /
shall be lawful.   F°. Broadside. **S.**

See No. 301.

Jan. 10. Plan of Inspector's Dept.

313. By the United States, in Congress assembled, / January 10, 1782. / Plan for conducting the 'Inspector's Department.
                                F°. Broadside.

In place of that adopted 25 Sept., 1780.

Jan. 24. Court Martial on Howe.

314. Proceedings / of a / General Court Mar-
tial, / Held at Philadelphia, / In the State of /
Pennsylvania, / By Order of his Excellency /
General Washington, / Commander in Chief /
of the Army of / The United States of Amer-
ica. / For the Trial of / Major General Howe, /
December 7, 1781. / Major General Baron Steu-
ben, President. / Philadelphia : / Printed by
Hall and Sellers, in Market-Street. / M.DCC.-
LXXXII. /   F°. pp. 31. **P.H.S.**

"February 15, 1782 . . . A letter of the 15th from major-
general R. Howe was read, requesting that the proceedings of the general court-martial on his trial be printed by
Congress." — *Journal.*

Feb. 23. Resolution on Exchange.

315. By the United States in Congress assembled. / February 20, 1782.
                        F°. Broadside. **V.S.**

Refusing to exchange "Charles, Earl Cornwallis," "not
from any apprehension of his influence or superior abili-
ties; but because they look upon him not in the light of a
British General, but a barbarian." It also relates to the
parole of Henry Laurens, and the maintenance of British
prisoners.

Aug. 7. Report on Expenditures.

316. By the United States in Congress assembled, Aug. 7, 1782.   4°. Broadside. **S.**

Report of a committee, consisting of Mr. Cornell, Mr.
Izard, Mr. Osgood, Mr. Bland, and Mr. Duane on the
"most just and practicable means of reducing the expenditures of the United States in the several departments."

Oct. 10. Notice to Contractors.

317. Office of Finance, October 10, 1782.
                        12°. Broadside. **P.L**

Public notice to contractors for continental supplies to
send in estimates for rations of 1783.

Oct. 18. Ordinance for Post Office.

318. General Post-Office, October 24th, 1782. /
Extract from an Ordinance passed by the United
States of America in Congress Assembled, Octo-
ber 18, 1782, entitled / An Ordinance for Regu-
lating the Post-Office of the United States of
America / [signed] James Bryson, Assistant.
                                F°. Broadside.

The draft of an ordinance erecting a post office was
reported to Congress by Mr. Scott, Mr. Clark and Mr.
Atlee, July 19, was read for a second time Oct. 2, and was
adopted Oct. 18, 1782.

Nov. 18. Receipts and Expenditures.

319. A general View of Receipts and Expenditures of Public Monies, by Authority from the
Superintendent of Finance, from the Time of
his entering on / the Administration of the

Finances, to the 31st December, 1781. / ..... /
[signed] Joseph Nourse, Register. / Register's
office, November 18, 1782. Oblong f°. Broadside.

Rules for Troops.

320. Rules and Articles / for the / Better
Government / of the / Troops raised, or to be
raised, / And kept in Pay, / By and at the Expense of the / United States / of / America. /
Philadelphia : Printed in the Year / 1782. /
                        Sm. 8°. pp. 39. **P.H.S.**

Title from *Hildeburn.*

Journals for 1781-2.

321. Journals / of / Congress, / and of the /
United States / in Congress Assembled. / For
the Year 1781. / Published by Order of Congress. / Volume VII. / Philadelphia : / Printed
by David C. Claypoole. / M,DCC.LXXXI.
                        8°. pp. 522, (4), lxxix. **P.L.**

Though the title is only for the year 1781, this volume
includes the whole of the year 1782. The supplementary
4 pages, or "Appendix to Volume seventh," is dated May
4, 1781, and are "Rules for conducting Business in the
United States in Congress assembled." The index is by
a misprint termed "General Index To Volume VIII."

322. Journals / of / Congress / and of the /
United States / in Congress assembled. / For
the Year 1781. / Published by order of Congress. /
Volume VII. / New York : / Printed by John
Patterson. / M,DCC.LXXXVII.
                        8°. pp. 522, (17), lxxix. **P.L.**

A reprint of the preceding volume, of which 500 copies
were printed by order of Congress of Sept. 13, 1786. It
follows that volume very closely, many pages being composed in exact copy, but it prints the report of Duane,
Sharp and Wolcott on the U. S. debts (Appendix pp. [5-
17]) which was not printed in the former volume, and the
error in the index is corrected.

1783.

Jan. 23. Proclamation of Treaty with Holland.

323. By the United States in Congress assembled : / A Proclamation / ..... / Done in
Congress this twenty-third day of Janu- / ary, in
the year of our Lord one thousand se- / ven
hundred and eighty-three, ... / ..... / Elias
Boudinot, President.   F°. 2 ll. **V.S.**

Jan. 31. Receipts and Expenditures.

324. A State of the Receipts and Expenditures
of Public Monies upon Warrants from the Superintendant of Finance, from the 1st of January
1782, / to the 1st of January 1783. / ..... /
[signed] Joseph Nourse, Register. / Register's
Office, January 31st, 1783.
                Oblong f°. Broadside. **S.D., V.S.**

Feb. 17. Resolution Concerning State Lands.
See under Apr. 18, 1783.

Mar. 18. Report of Committee on Impost.

325. March 18, 1783. / Resolved / That it be
recommended to the several states, / .. / :.. /
... / ... to invest in the United States in / Congress assembled, a power to levy for the use of
the / United States, the following duties upon
goods ...
                F°. 2 lls. (on one side only.) **S.D.**

In the copy examined, "March" was stricken out from
the title, and April substituted in Ms.
A report made by Gorham, Hamilton, Madison, Fitz-
simons, and Rutledge.
See under Apr. 18, 1783.

Apr. 11. Treaty with England.

326. By the / United States of America / In Congress assembled / A Proclamation, / Declaring the Cessation of Arms, as / well by Sea as by Land, Agreed upon / between the United States of Ame- / rica and his Britannic Majesty; and / enjoining the Observance thereof. / ..... / Done in Congress, at Philadelphia, this Eleventh Day / of April, in / the Year of Our Lord One Thousand Seven / Hundred and Eighty-three. / ..... / [signed] / Elias Boudinot, President / ..... / Richmond: Printed by James Hayes, Printer to the Commonwealth.

F°. Broadside. V.S.

Followed by a proclamation by Governor Harrison. This is the preliminary treaty.

Apr. 18. Resolution Concerning State Lands and Impost.

327. By the United States in / Congress assembled. / February 17, 1783.

F°. 2 ll. P.L., V.S.

The resolution adopted Feb. 17, for surveying lands, and that of Apr. 18, advising the States to grant power to levy an impost.

Apr. 18. Resolutions on Impost.

328. Resolved, that it be recommended to the several / states, as indispensably necessary to the restoration of / public [sic] credit ... / .. to vest in the united / states in congress assembled, a power to levy for the / use of the united states, a duty of five per centum ad / valorem, ...

F°. 3 ll. [on one side only.] S.D.

The resolutions concerning the impost. See under Mar. 18, 1783.

Apr. 24. Address and Recommendations.

329. Address / and / Recommendations / to / The States, / by / The United States in Congress / assembled. / Philadelphia: / Printed by David C. Claypoole. / M,DCC,LXXXIII.

8°. pp. 14, (1), 9, (1), 3, 6, 5, 4, 20. B.A.
8°. pp. 14, (1), 9, (1), 3, 6, 5, 4. 26. P.L.

There are two editions of this pamphlet; with the difference in collation noted above. They are identical in matter to the ninth page of the last division, where a foot note, partially filling pp. 9–16, is added. There are also variations in the composing of the types.

A Circular Letter to the States, on the necessity of raising revenues for the general government, reported by James Madison, Hamilton, and Oliver Ellsworth.

The accompanying papers include Hamilton's report on the refusal of R. I to agree to the impost, the French and Dutch contracts, the Address to Congress from the officers of the Continental Army, The "Newburgh Addresses," written by John Armstrong, and the Congressional resolutions of Sept. 6 and Oct. 10, 1780, Dec. 16, 1782, and Feb. 17, 1783.

"The evidence of Mr. Madison's sentiments at one period, is to be found in the address of Congress, of Apr. twenty sixth [sic] seventeen hundred and eighty three, which was planned by him, in conformity to his own ideas, and without any previous suggestions from the committee."—*Hamilton to Carrington*, May 26, 1792.

330. Address / and / Recommendations / to / The States, / by / The United States in Congress / assembled. / Philadelphia: / Printed 1783. / Boston: Reprinted, / By Order of the Hon. House of Representatives of the / Commonwealth of Massachusetts, 1783.

8°. pp. 62. B.A.

331. Address / and / Recommendations / to / The States, / by / The United States in Congress / assembled. / Philadelphia, Printed: /

Hartford: Re-printed by Hudson & Goodwin, / M,DCC,LXXXIII.

4°. pp. 50, 31, folding table. P.L.

The additional pages are detailed accounts of Connecticut finances.

332. By order of Congress. / Addresses / and / Recommendations / to the / States, / by the / United States / in Congress assembled. / Philadelphia: / Printed by David C. Claypoole. / London: reprinted / For J. Stockdale, in Piccadilly. / M,DCC,LXXXIII. 8°. pp. 91, (1). P.L.

333. Address / and / Recommendations / to / The States, / by / The United States in Congress / Assembled. / Richmond: / Printed by Nicholson and Prentis / M,DCC,LXXXIII.

8°. pp. 60, and more. C.

334. Address / and / Recommendations / to / The States, / by / The United States in Congress / assembled. / Trenton: / Re-Printed by Isaac Collins, / M,DCC,LXXXIII.

12°. pp. 56. N.J.H.S.

June 24. Proclamation on Mutiny of Pa. Line.

335. By His Excellency, / Elias Boudinot, Esquire, / President of the United States in Congress Assembled, / A Proclamation. / ..... / Philadelphia, Printed by David C. Claypoole.

F°. Broadside. L.C.P.

Sept. 13. Report on Virginia Cession of Land.

336. The committee, to whom were referred the act / of the legislature of Virginia, of the 2d of Ja- / nuary, 1781, and the report thereon, report ... / F°. Broadside. S.D., V.S.

Reported by John Rutledge, Ellsworth, Bedford, Gorham, and Madison. The original draft is in Rutledge's handwriting.

Sept. 22. Proclamation in re Indian Lands.

337. By the United States in Congress / Assembled. / A Proclamation. / Philadelphia: Printed by David C. Claypoole.

F°. 1 l. L.C.P.

Sept. 25. Proclamation of Treaty with Sweden.

338. By the United States in Congress Assembled, A Proclamation ... Princeton, September 25th, 1783. Elias Boudinot, President.

F°.

Lot 675, "Washington relics," Catalogue, Apr. 21, 1891.

Oct. 15. Report on Indian Affairs.

339. The committee, consisting of Mr. Duane, Mr. / Peters, Mr. Carrol, [sic] Mr. Hawkins and Mr. Lee. / to whom was referred a report on Indian af- / fairs, [etc.] ..... submit the following detail of facts and resolutions : — /

F°. Broadside of 2 columns. S.D.

Oct. 15. Additional Report on Indian Affairs.

340. The committee consisting of Mr. Duane, Mr. Peters, / Mr. Carroll, Mr. Hawkins and Mr. A. Lee. to / whom were referred a report on Indian affairs, and the / several other papers. ..... / beg leave to subjoin the following additional instructions / and propositions to their said former report:

F°. Broadside of 2 columns. S.D.

Nov. 1. Resolutions on Congressional Representation.

341. By the United States in / Congress Assembled. / November 1, 1783.

F°. Broadside. S.D., V.S.

Half-Pay and Commutation.

342. A / Collection of Papers, / relative to / Half-Pay / and / Commutation / of / Half-Pay, / granted By / Congress / to the / Officers of the Army. / Compiled, / By Permission of His Excellency General Washington, / from the Original Papers in his Possession. / Fish-kill: / Printed by Samuel Loudon. / M,DCC.LXXXIII. 8°. pp. 36.

343. The / Last Official / Address, / of his Excellency / General Washington, / to the / Legislature of the United States. / To which is annexed, / A Collection of Papers relative to / Half-Pay, / and Commutation of / Half-Pay. / Granted by Congress to the / Officers of the Army. / Hartford: / Printed by Hudson and Goodwin. / M.DCC.LXXXIII. 8°. pp. 48. **N.**

344. A / Collection of Papers, / relative to / Half-Pay, / and / Commutation thereof, / granted by / Congress / to the / Officers of the Army. / Together with a / Circular Letter / from / His Excellency General Washington, / to the several / Legislatures of the United States. / Boston: / Printed by Order of the General Court / of the Commonwealth of Massachusetts. / M,DCC,-LXXXIII. 4°. pp. 24. **B.A.**

Journals. 1782-3.

345. Journal / of the / United States / In Congress Assembled, / containing / The Proceedings / from / The First Monday in November 1782, / to / The First Monday in November 1783. / Volume VIII. / Published by order of Congress. / Philadelphia: / Printed by David C. Claypoole. / M,DCC,LXXXIII. 8°. pp. 483.

1784.

Jan. 14. Proclamation of English Treaty.

346. By the United States in / Congress Assembled, / January 14, 1784. 4°. Broadside. **V.S.**

The proclamation of the definitive treaty with England, signed by Thomas Mifflin.

Mar. 1. Government of North West Territory.

347. The Committee appointed to prepare a Plan for the tem- / porary Government of the Western Territory, have / agreed to the following Resolutions. F°. 1 l. **S.D., H.S.P.**

Reported by Jefferson, Chase, and Howell, the draft being in the handwriting of the former. On Mar. 17 it was recommitted. See following title.

Mar. 22. Report on North West Territory.

348. The Committee to whom was recommitted the Report of a / Plan for a temporary Government of the Western Ter- / ritory, have agreed to the following Resolutions. / ..... F°. Broadside. **S.D.**

The draft is in Jefferson's handwriting.

Mar. 23, 1784. Resolution on Qualifications.

349. By the United States in / Congress assembled. / March 23, 1784. F°. Broadside. **P.L.**

Adopted in consequence of the report of Sherman, Jefferson, Beatty, Chase, and Williamson.

Apr. 5. Report on Finances.

350. The Grand Committee consisting of [blank] / appointed to prepare and report to Congress, the arrears of interest on the national / debt, together with the interest and expenses for the year 1784, from the first to the last / day

thereof inclusive, and a requisition of money on the states for discharging the / same, have agreed to the following Report: / F°. Broadside. **P.L.**

The committee consisted of Jefferson, Blanchard, Gerry, Howell, Sherman, De Witt, Dick, Hand, Stone, Williamson, and Read. The draft is in Jefferson's handwriting. See under Apr. 27, 1784.

Apr. 22. Report on Commercial Affairs.

351. The Committee to whom was referred sundry Letters / and Papers relative to Commercial Matters, submit the follow- / ing circular Letter and Resolves. F°. Broadside. **S.D., P.L.**

Reported by Gerry, Read, Williamson, Chase, and Jefferson. Consid. red Apr. 30. See No. 354.

Apr. 23. Land Office Ordinance.

See under May 20, 1785.

Apr. 27. Report on Finances.

352. The United States in Congress assembled. / April 27, 1784. / F°. Broadside.

The report of the grand committee (see No. 350) as amended and adopted by the Congress.

353. The / United States / in / Congress assembled, / April 27, 1784. / Congress resumed the considera- / tion of the report to the Grand / Committee appointed to pre- / pare and report to Congress, the arrears / of Interest on the national debt, toge- / ther with the expenses for the year / 1784, from the first to the last day / thereof inclusive, and a requisition of / money on the States for maintaining the / same, which being amended to read as follows; / ..... / [colophon]. Boston: Printed by Adams and Nourse. / By Order of the Honourable House of Representatives. / M,DCC,XXXIV. 8°. pp. 12. **M.**

Apr. 30. Resolutions on Commerce.

354. By the United States / in Congress assembled. April 30, 1784. F°. Broadside. **S.D.**

See under Apr. 22, 1784.

May 6. Report on Western Posts.

355. The Committee consisting of Mr. Mercer, Mr. / Lee, Mr. Gerry, Mr. Howell and Mr. [E] Paine, " appointed to / consider of the measures proper to be adopted in order / to take possession of the frontier posts," having considered / the same, and sundry papers to them referred, thereon beg / leave to observe — ... / F°. Broadside. **S.D.**

Considered May 12, 1784.

May 17. Report on Continental Bills.

356. The Grand Committee to whom was referred / a Letter of the Governor of Massachusetts, of the 28th of Oc- / tober, 1783, relative to the Continental Bills of Credit / of / the Old Emissions, submit the following. / 4°. Broadside. **P.L.**

Agreed to in Committee Apr. 7, and laid before Congress May 17, 1784. It was apparently never considered. The draft is in Jefferson's handwriting.

May 28. Report on Southern Indians.

357. The Committee consisting of Mr. Beresford, Mr. Jefferson, Mr. / Chase, Mr. Spaight and Mr. Read, appointed to take into consider- / ation the / state of Indian affairs in the Southern department, beg leave to Report: / F°. pp. (3). **S.D.**

Drafted by Jefferson.

June 3. Report on Accounts.

358. The Committee consisting of Mr. Spaight, Mr. Gerry, Mr. Lee, / Mr. Beatty, and Mr. Sherman, to whom was referred a report of a committee on a re- / port of the superintendant of finance, dated the 5th of November, 1783, ... / ..... / ... / submit to Congress the fol- / lowing Report. / Fº. Broadside. S.D.

Oct. 22. Treaty with Six Nations.

359. Articles of a Treaty, / Concluded at Fort Stanwix. on the twenty-second day of October, one / thousand seven hundred and eighty-four, / between Oliver Wolcott, Richard / Butler and Arthur Lee, Commissioners Plenipotentiary from / the United States in Congress assembled, on the one Part, and the Sachems / and Warriors of the Six Nations on the other. Fº. 1 l. P.L.

Consular Convention.

360. The / Scheme / of / a Convention, / Between His Most Christian Majesty and the United States of North Ame- / rica, for defining and regulating the Functions and Privileges of Con- / suls, Vice-Consuls, Agents and Commissaries. / ..... Fº. pp. 11. S.D.

Agreed to between Vergennes and Franklin, and transmitted by the latter to Congress, which refused to ratify it. This is a translation by John Pintard. See Nos. 383, 395 and 467.

Reports on Penobscot Expedition.

361. The Grand Committee consisting of Mr. / Stone, Mr. Blanchard, Mr. Gerry, Mr. Howell, Mr. Sher- / man, Mr. De Witt, Mr. Dick, Mr. Hand, Mr. Hardy, / Mr. Williamson and Mr. Read, to whom were referred / an act of the legislature of Connecticut, and a letter from the governor of Massachusetts respecting the ex- / pences of / that state in an expedition against the British forces at Pe- / nobscot, and other matters, submit the following resolves. / [second] The Grand Committee to whom was referred / a letter of the governor of Massachusetts, of the 28th of / October 1783, relative to the continental bills of credit / of the old emissions, submit the following. / Fº. Broadside. S.D.

Collection of Treaties.

362. A / Collection / of / Papers : / containing / The Declaration of Independence of the / United States of America, dated July 4th, 1776. / The Treaties of Alliance and Commerce, between / the United States of America and France, Feb. 6, 1778. / Transcript of the Treaty between France and the / United States of America, July 16th, 1782; with the / Ratification thereof by Congress. / The Treaty of Amity and commerce, between the / States General of the United Netherlands and the / United States of America, dated October 8th, 1782, / with the Ratification thereof by Congress. / The Decree of the Queen of Portugal for opening a / Commercial Intercourse between her Subjects and those / of the United States of America, dated Febr. 13. 1783. / Treaty of Amity and Commerce between his Maje- / sty The King of Sweden, and the United States of Ame- / rica, dated April 3. 1783; with the Ratification there- / of by Congress. / Defin- / itive Treaty of Peace between the United / States of America and his Britannic Majesty, dated / September 3d. 1783; with the ratification thereof / by Congress. / To which is added / His Excel-

lency General Washington's Circular Letter / to the different Governors of the respective States, dated / June 11, 1783. / New York : / Printed by Samuel Loudon. [1784] 12º. pp. 96. N.

Feb. 8. Report on Invalids.

363. The Committee consisting of Mr. M'Henry, Mr. Dick, / and Mr. Williamson, to whom was referred a motion of Mr. / M'Henry, respecting Invalids, submit the following Resolves. / Fº. Broadside. S.D.

Journals. 1783-4.

364. Journal / of the / United States / In Congress Assembled : / containing / The Proceedings / from / The Third Day of November, 1783, / to / The Third Day of June, 1784. / Volume IX. / Published by order of Congress. / Philadelphia : / Printed by John Dunlap, / Printer to the United States in / Congress Assembled. / 8º. pp. 317, xviii, 47.

The last 47 pages are the Journal of the Committee of the States, the title of which is as follows :—

Journal of the Committee of States.

365. Journal / of the / Committee of The States : / containing / The Proceedings / from / The First Friday in June, 1784, / to / The Second Friday in August, 1784. / Published by order of Congress. / Printed by John Dunlap. / Printer to the United States in / Congress Assembled. / M,DCC,LXXXIV. 8º. pp. 47.

1785.

Jan. 21. Treaty with Indians.

366. Articles of a Treaty, / Concluded at Fort M'Intosh, the 21st day of January 1785, between / the Commissioners Plenipotentiary of the United States of Ame- / rica of the one part, and the Sachems and Warriors of the Wiandot, Dela- / ware, Chippawa and Ottawa Nations of the other. / Fº. 1 l. P.L.

Feb. 2. Proclamation in re Counterfeits.

367. Proclamation / By the United States in Con- / gress assembled / ..... / [signed] Richard Henry Lee. Fº. Broadside. S.

Feb. 23. Report on Accounts.

368. The Committee consisting of Mr. Williamson, Mr. Stewart / and Mr. Hardy, to whom were referred a Letter from the Su- / preme Executive of the State of Pennsylvania, dated 20th De- / cember; a Letter dated 24th January, from William Denning, / Esquire, Auditor of Accounts ; and sundry other Letters and Papers — beg leave to report, / Fº. Broadside. S.D.

The following was adopted, as the result of this report :—

Feb. 23. Resolutions on Accounts.

369. By the United States in Con- / gress assembled. / February 23, 1785. Fº. Broadside. S.

Mar. 11. Report on Southern Indians.

370. The Committee consisting of Mr. Hardy, Mr. Houston, Mr. Read, / Mr. Williamson, and Mr. Holten, to whom was referred the Report of a / Committee on the State of Southern Indian Affairs, beg / leave to submit the following Report. / Fº. Broadside. P.L.

Agreed to, Mar. 15, 1785.

Mar. 14. French Duties.

371. State / of the / Duties / Payable by Vessels of the / United States / of / America, / In the Ports of Marseilles, Bayonne, l'Orient, / and Dunkirk. / Published by Order of the Honorable John Jay, Esquire, / Secretary of the United States, for the Department of / Foreign Affairs. / New-York: / Printed and Sold by F. Childs and Co. No. 17 Duke-Street.

F°. pp. 19. **V.S., S.D.**

Mar. 17. Report on Accounts.

372. The Committee consisting of Mr. Gerry, Mr. William- / son and Mr. Hardy, to whom were referred a Motion of / Mr. Gerry, and a Motion of Mr. Howell, submit the fol- / lowing Resolves. F°. Broadside. **S.D.**

Mar. 18. Report on Secretary of Congress.

373. The Committee consisting of Mr. Howell, Mr. Monroe, Mr. Pinck- / ney, Mr. R. R. Livingston and Mr. Gardner, appointed to revise the Insti- / tution of the Office of the Secretary of Congress, and to report such Altera- / tions as they may judge necessary, — beg leave to report the following Draft / of an Ordinance, / An Ordinance for the Regulation of the Office of [MS. "the"] Secretary of / Congress, and for extending it to the Home Department.

F°. Broadside. **S.D.**

Discussed and amended after its introduction, and adopted on Mar. 31, as follows: —

Mar. 31. Ordinance of Secretary of Congress.

374. By the United States in / Congress assembled / March 31, 1785. / An Ordinance for the Regulation of the Office / of the Secretary of Congress. / F°. Broadside. **P.L., V.S.**

Apr. 1. Report on Western Posts.

375. The Committee to whom was referred a Motion of Mr. / R. R. Livingston, and two Motions of Mr. Monroe, relative to / the Western Posts, together with a Letter from Major / North, — submit the following Report. /

F°. Broadside. **S.D.**

Considered on Apr. 1 and 7. From the reference to the letter of North, under date of Mar. 22, in the *Journals*, the committee was apparently Ellery, Howell, and Williamson.

Apr. 6. Report on Slavery.

376. The Committee consisting of, &c. to whom was refer- / red a Motion of Mr. King, for the Exclusion of invo- / luntary Servitude in the States described in the Resolve of Con- / gress of the 23d Day of April, 1784, submit the following Resolve. / .....

4°. Broadside. **S.D.**

King made his motion Mar. 16, 1785, and it was committed the same day to a committee composed of King, Howell, and Ellery. This is their report, recommending the limitation of slavery in the North West to the period before 1801, and for the return of fugitive slaves. It was apparently never acted upon.

Apr. 15. Report on Finances.

377. The Grand Committee to whom was re- / ferred a letter from the superintendant of finance of the 29th of April / last, ... submit the following / resolves / ..... F°. Broadside. **S.D.**

Apr. 18. Report on Landais.

378. The Committee to whom was referred the Memorial / of Mr. P. Landais. Report,

F°. 1 l. **P.L., S.D.**

May. Report on Money.

379. Propositions respecting the Coinage / of Gold, Silver, and Copper.

F°. pp. 12. **S.D.**

The report of the "grand committee," consisting of Howell, Foster, King, Cook, Smith, Beatty, Gardner, Vining, Hindman, Monroe, Williamson, Pinckney, and Houston, with the plan of Robert Morris, (written by Gouverneur Morris) dated January 15, 1782, and "Notes on the Establishment of a Money Mint, and of a Coinage for the United States. By Mr. Jefferson." In consequence of this report, Congress, on July 6, 1785, adopted the dollar as the unit of coinage, and the decimal ratio.

May 20. Land Office Ordinance.

380. By the United States in Con- / gress Assembled. / April 23. 1784. / [second leaf] May 20, 1785. / An Ordinance for ascertaining the Mode of disposing of Lands / in the Western Territory. F°. 2 ll. **V.S.**

On Apr. 23, 1784, a committee consisting of Jefferson, Williamson, Howell, Gerry, and Read, reported "an ordinance establishing a Land Office for the United States," which had been drafted by Jefferson. It was read on Apr. 30, and postponed till May 7, when, according to the *Journal*, it was read for the first time, and May 10 assigned for its consideration. It was not again taken up till May 28, 1784, when the motion to consider was negatived. It was apparently again taken up on Mar. 4, 1785, and, on Mar. 16, was referred to a committee of a member of each state, consisting of Long, King, Howell, Johnson, Livingston, Stewart, Gardner, Henry, Grayson, Bull, and Houston. They reported "an Ordinance for ascertaining the mode of disposing of lands in the western territory," on Apr. 12, the draft being written by William Grayson. This was considered on Apr. 14, 20, 22, 25, 26, being printed in the *Journal* of the latter day, and on May 20 was read a third time and adopted.

June 7. Resolutions on Soldiers and Sailors.

381. By the United States in Congress / Assembled. / June 7, 1785.

F°. Broadside. **P.L.**

June 15. Report on Indian Treaties.

382. The Committee to whom was referred the Letters of the Commissioners authorised to form Treaties with the In- / dian Tribes, having conferred with the said Commissioners / upon the subject of their Letter, and the Resolutions of 18th of March, / directing a Treaty to be held at Port St. Vincent, on the [blank] / day of June next, Report, / F°. 1 l. **S.D.**

July 4. Report on Consular Convention.

383. Office for Foreign Affairs, July 4, 1785. / The Secretary of the United States / for the Department of Foreign Affairs, to whom was re- / ferred a Copy of the Convention respecting French and / American Consuls, Reports, / ..... / [signed] John Jay F°. pp. 9. **S.D.**

See No. 360 and 395.

July 13. Report on Commerce.

384. The Committee consisting of [blank] to whom was referred the / Motion of Mr. Monroe, submit the following Report. / .... / F°. Broadside. **S.D.**

The committee was Monroe, Spaight, Houston, Johnson, and King.

July 18. Report on Supplies.

385. The Grand Committee to whom was re- committed a Report on the Subject of Supplies for the Year One / Thousand Seven Hundred and Eighty-five, submit the following Report. F°. Broadside. **S.D.**

The committee was Howell, Foster, King, Cook, Smith, Dick, Pettit, Hindman, Monroe, Pinckney, and Baldwin.

July 27. Resolution on State Laws.

386. By the United States in / Congress assembled / July 27, 1785. /
F°. Broadside. P.L., D.S., S.
Moved by Gerry.

Aug. 17. Representation in Congress.

387. By the United States / in Congress assembled. / August 17, 1785.
F°. Broadside. V.S., S.
Adopted in consequence of a report by Gerry, Hardy, and Pinckney. It provides that a monthly return of the attendance of the delegates be transmitted to each state. The following was accordingly printed and used for this purpose: —

Aug. 17. Representation in Congress.

388. A State of the Representation in Congress for the Month / of [blank] 178 [blank] pursuant to the Act of the 7th August, 1785.
F°. Broadside. S.

Aug. 27. Loan Offices.

389. Board of Treasury, / August 27, 1785. / ..... / [signed] Samuel Osgood, / Walter Livingston.
F°. 1 l. S.D.
Report on the Continental Loan Offices.

Sept. 27. Requisitions for 1785.

390. By the United States in / Congress assembled / September 27, 1785.
F°. 2 ll. S.

Sept. 29. Marine Ordinance.

391. Office for Foreign Affairs, 29th September, 1785. / The Secretary of the United States, for the Department of Foreign / Affairs, in Obedience to the Order of Congress, reports the Draft of an Ordinance for the Trial of Piracies and Felonies committed on / the High Seas. /
F°. 2 ll.
Prepared by John Jay.

Sept. 30. Duties of Loan Officers.

392. By the United States in / Congress assembled, / September 30, 1785.
F°. 1 l. S.

Oct. 3.

393. By the United States in Con- / gress assembled / October 3, 1785.
F°. Broadside. S.

Oct. 12. Resolution on Quotas.

394. By the United States in / Congress assembled, / October 12, 1785.
F°. Broadside. S.
Moved by Gerry.

Oct. 13. Report on Consuls.

395. Office for Foreign Affairs, / October 13, 1785. / The Secretary of the United States for the Depart- / ment of Foreign Affairs, to whom was referred back / his Report of the 19th ult. respecting Consuls, accompanied with a motion of the same date; / Reports, / ..... / [signed] John Jay.
F°. Broadside. S.D., P.L.
See Nos. 360 and 395.

Nov. 2.

396. By the United States in / Congress assembled / November 2, 1785.
F°. Broadside. S.

Report of Grand Committee.

397. The Grand Committee consisting of Mr. / Foster, Mr. Gerry, Mr. Howell, Mr. Cook, Mr. Lawrence, Mr. Cad- / wallader, Mr. Pettit, Mr. Hindman, Mr. Hardy, Mr. Cumming, Mr. /

Read and Mr. Houstoun, to whom were committed sundry Motions, / Report, / .....
F°. 1 l. S.D.

Report on Pollock.

398. The Committee consisting of Mr. Ger- / ry, Mr. Ellery and Mr. Wilson, to whom was re ferred a Petition / and sundry Papers of Mr. Oliver Pollock, late an Agent of the / United States at Havannah, submit the following Report.
F°. Broadside. S.D.

Accounts of Morris.

399. A Statement of the Accounts of the United States ..... during the administration of the Superintendent of Finance Commencing with his Appointment on the 20th ..... of February, 1781, and Ending with the Resignation. on the 1st ..... of November, 1784. Philadelphia: Printed by Robert Aitken. M,DCC.LXXXV. F°.
Printed by Morris as a justification of his management of the finances. The following relates to the same subject : —

Accounts of Morris.

400. Statements / of the / Receipts and Expenditures / of Public Money, / During the Administration of the Finances. / By Robert Morris, Esquire, / late Superintendant. / With the Extracts and Accounts from the Public Records, / Made out by the Register of the Treasury. / By Direction of the House of Representatives, / appointed by an order of the House, / Of the 19th of March 1790, Upon the Memorial of the Said late Superintendant of Finances. /
F°. pp. 56, 4, 14.

Sample of Journal.

401. Journal of Congress. 241 [1785]
F°. Broadside. S.D.
.*. A specimen leaf, accompanying Dunlap's proposition for printing the Journals in folio.

Journal. 1784-5.

402. Journal / of the / United States / In Congress Assembled: / Containing / The Proceedings / from / The First Monday in November, 1784. / Published by order of Congress. / Printed by John Dunlap. / Printer to the United States in / Congress Assembled. / M,DCC,LXXXV.
8°. pp. 368.

1786.

Jan. 4. Report on Revenues and Commerce.

403. By the United States in / Congress assembled. / Jan. 2, 1786.
F°. 2 ll. P.L.
A resolution of Congress, of Jan. 2, calling on the Secretary of Congress for information concerning public measures, and his reply, dated Jan. 4.

Feb. 9. Report on Finances.

404. The report of a Committee, ap- / pointed to consider whether any and what Measures / may be necessary for Congress to adopt, in pursuance / of their Recommendations to the se- / veral States on the 18th of April, 1783.
F°. Broadside. P.L.
Made by Monroe, Johnson, Symmes, and Livermore.

Feb. 15. Report on Impost.

405. The Committee, consisting of Mr. King, Mr. / Pinckney, Mr. Kean, Mr. Monroe, and Mr. Pettit, to whom were referred several / Reports and Documents concerning the System of Gen-

eral / Revenue, recommended by Congress on
the 18th of April, 1783, — / Report, / .....
F°. 1 l. **S.D.**

Mar. 3. Report on Import.

406. United States in Congress assembled, /
March 3, 1786.　　　F°. Broadside. **S.D.**
Made by Kean, Gorham, Pinckney, Smith, and Gray-
son.

Mar. 8. Resolution on Western Territory.

407. Motion / of / Mr. Dane, / .....
F°. Broadside. **S.D.**

Mar. 18. Report on Militia.

408. A / Plan / for the / General Arrangement / of the / Militin / of the / United States. /
The regulations for the discipline and government / of the Militia, will be submitted here-
after. /　　　　S°. pp. 34. **B.A.**
The introductory matter (pages 1-2) precedes this title
page, and is signed " H. Knox, War-Office, 18th March,
1786."

Mar. 24. Report on Departments.

409. The Committee, consisting of / Mr.
Pinckney, Mr. Dane, Mr. Monroe, Mr. Johnson
/ and Mr. King, to whom were referred a Report from / the Board of Treasury, on revising
the system adopted / for the Settlement of the
Accounts of the Five / Great Departments, and
containing such Alterations therein, as would, in
their opinion, / be more conducive to a speedy
and just Settlement of / the said Accounts —
recommend it be / Resolved, ...
F°. Broadside. **S.D.**

Apr. 8. Plan of Mint.

410. (1) / Board of Treasury, April 8, 1786.
4°. pp. 28. **S.D.**
Reports on a Mint, and coinage, by S. Osgood and
Walter Livingston. See No. 416.

May 17. Treaty with Prussia.

411. The United States in Congress assembled : / To all whom these Presents shall
come Greeting.　　F°. Broadside. **S.**

May ? Report on Confederation.

412. A Motion of Mr. Dane / That a Committee of five be appointed to examine how far
the several States / have complied with, and
adopted the Alteration of the Eighth Article of
the / Confederation and perpetual Union, recommended by Congress, April 18, 1783, / and to
consider and report, what further Measures are
proper to be adopted by Con- / gress, for carry-
ing into Effect a Federal Rule for apportioning
Federal Taxes / on the several States. / The
Committee consisting of Mr. Dane, Mr. Grayson, Mr. Mitchell, Mr. Monroe, and Mr. Kean,
to whom was referred the Motion of Mr. Dane, /
of February 27, 1786, ... / Report ...
F°. 1 l. **S.D.**
There is nothing to settle the date of this report by, but
it was clearly made in the latter part of April, or in May,
1786.

May 31. Report on Articles of War.

413. The Committee consisting of Mr. St.
Clair, / Mr. Lee and Mr. Lawrence, to whom
was referred a Report of / the Secretary at War,
on the Articles of War and Court-Mar- / tial report as follows : ...　　F°. 2 ll. **P.L.**

Considered and adopted on the above date. They are
rules for the administration of justice in the army, and
were embodied in subsequent editions of the " Rules and
Articles."

June 16. Report on Congress.

414. Your Committee beg leave to Report. —
F°. Broadside. **S.D.**
Endorsed " Lee King Kean to report the power which
Congress may rightfully exercise to compel the attendance
of the members." " Sixty Copies receiv'd June 16, 1786.
Printed by Mr. Swain."

June ? Report on Indian Ordinance.

415. The Committee consisting of Mr. Pinckney, Mr. Morse, and Mr. King, appointed to
form / an Ordinance for the complent Arrangement and Government of the Indian Depart- /
ment, — submit the following to the consideration of Congress. — / An Ordinance for Regulating the Indian Department.　F°. 1 l. **S.D.**
According to the endorsement, this was made in June.
The first mention of it in the printed *Journals* is under
July 20, when Congress " resumed the consideration " of
it. See under Aug. 7, 1786.

June 22. Report of Board of Treasury.

416. Board of Treasury, June 22, 1786 [at
end] Samuel Osgood, Walter Livingston Arthur
Lee.　　　　　F°. 2 ll. **P.L.**
A report on the requisitions for the year.

June 27. Resolutions on Court of Appeal.

417. By the United States, / in Congress assembled, / June 27, 1786.　F°. Broadside. **S.**

July 1. Receipts and Expenditures.

418. General Account of the Receipts and Expenditures of the United States / From 1st December, 1785, to 30th June 1786. / ..... / July
1, 1786. / J. Nourse.　F°. Broadside. **V.S., S.**

July 7. Report on Western Territory.

419. The grand Committee, consisting of /
[blank] to whom were, / among other Things,
referred a motion of Mr. Monroe, respecting the
Ces- / sions and Division of Western Lands and
/ Territory, — / Report, —
F°. Broadside. **S.D.**

July 14. Resolutions on Delegates.

420. By the United States in / Congress assembled. / July 14th, 1786.　F°. Broadside.

July 26. Draft of Indian Ordinance.

421. An Ordinance, &c. F°. Broadside. **S.D.**
For the regulation of Indian affairs.

Aug. 2. Requisitions for 1786.

422. By the United States in / Congress assembled. / August 2, 1786. F°. 1 l. **S.D., S.**
See No. 416.

Aug. 7. Indian Ordinance.

423. By the United States in / Congress assembled. / August 7, 1786 / An Ordinance for
the Regulation of Indian Affairs.
F°. 1 l. **S., S.D.**

Aug. 22. Report on Impost.

424. The Committee, consisting of Mr. Johnson, Mr. King, Mr. Pinckney, Mr. Monroe and
Mr. Grayson, to / whom was referred a Letter

from his Excellency the Governor of New-York, of the 16th instant, — / Report, — / .....
F°. Broadside. S.D.

Adopted Aug. 23.

Sept. 18. **Resolutions on Loan Offices.**

425. By the United States in / Congress assembled / September 18, 1786.
F°. Broadside. P.L.

Sept. 20. **Report on Mint.**

426. An Ordinance for the Establishment of the Mint of the United / States of America; and for Regulating the Value and Alloys of Coin. / ..... / [signed] Samuel Osgood, / Arthur Lee. / Board of Treasury, September 20, 1786.
F°. 1 l. S.D.

Reported in pursuance of an order of Congress, of Aug. 8. See Nos. 409 and 429.

Sept. 21. **Report on North West Territory.**

427. The Committee, consisting of Mr. Johnson, Mr. Pinckney, Mr. Smith, Mr. Dane and Mr. / Henry, appointed to prepare a Plan of a Temporary Government for / such Districts, or new States, as shall be laid out by the United States, upon the Principles of / the Acts of Cession from individual States, and admitted into the Confederacy, — / Submit the following Report to the Consideration of Congress. / .....
F°. 1 l. S.D.

Considered Sept. 29 and Oct. 4.

Oct. 13. **Ordinance for Liquidation.**

428. An Ordinance for Establishing a Board, to Li- / quidate and Settle all Accounts between the Uni- / ted States, and the Individual States.
F°. Broadside. V.S.

On Oct. 5 Congress considered the report of a committee, consisting of Smith, Long, Johnson, Bull, Carrington, Henry, and Kean, to whom this subject had been referred, in consequence of motions of King and the delegates of Virginia. It was again considered on the 9, 12, and 13 of October, on the latter day being agreed to.

Oct. 16. **Ordinance of Mint.**

429. An Ordinance for the Establishment of the Mint / of the United States of America, and for regula- / ting the value of alloy of Coin. /
F°. Broadside. S.

See Nos. 409 and 426.

Oct. 20. **Report on Indians.**

430. By the United States in / Congress assembled. / October 20, 1786. / The Committee consisting of Mr. Pettit, Mr. Lee, Mr. Pinckney, / Mr. Henry and Mr. Smith, to whom was referred the Letter from / the War Office with Papers enclosed containing Intelligence / of the hostile Intentions of the Indians in the Western Coun- / try having Reported :
F°. Broadside. V.S.

Oct. 23. **Report on State Laws.**

431. By the United States in Con- / gress assembled. / October 23, 1786. / The Committee, consisting of Mr. Pinckney, Mr. Smith and Mr. Henry, to whom was / referred an Act of the Legislature of the State of Georgia, Passed in consequence of the Resolution of / the 30th April, respecting Commerce, and the Subject of said Recommendations, having Re- / ported —
F°. Broadside. V.S., S.D.

Foreign Loans.

432. Schedule of the French and Dutch / Loans, / Shewing the Periods of their Redemp-

tion, with the annual Interest payable thereon until their final Ex- / tinction, for which Provision is yet to be made.
F°. 1 l. S.D.

Loan Office.

433. Resolution and Extracts / From the / Journal of the Honorable the Congress, / relative to the Continental Loan-Offices / in the several States; / and / certain Letters, passed between Robert / Morris, Esq; Superintendant of Finance — / the Board of Treasury of the United / States / and / Abraham Yates, Jun. Esq; late Commis- / sioner of the Continental Loan Office of / the State of New-York. / Printed at Albany, by Charles R. Webster, No. 36 State-street near the English Church. /
M.DCC.LXXXVI 12mo. pp. 31.

Printed by Abraham Yates, as a personal vindication of himself. Cf. *Journals* for 1786, pages 68, 69; for 1787, page 187.

Accounts.

434. Accounts of the U. S. with the States. / 1786 / Dr. and Cr.
F°. pp. 82. B.A.

Prepared by J. Nourse.

Journal. 1786.

435. Journal / of the / United States / In Congress Assembled : / containing the / Proceedings / from / The 3d Day of November, 1785. / To / The 3d Day of November, 1786. / Volume XII. / Published by Order of Congress. / Printed by John Dunlap. 8°. pp. 267, xvi.

Both the title-page and index style this volume XII, though really XI.

1787.

Jan. 1. **Schedule of Requisitions.**

436. Schedule of Requisitions on the several States by the United States in Congress assembled ; / Of 10th Sept. 1782 — 30th Oct. 1781, and 27th and 28th April, 1784 — Of the 27th Sept. 1785, — and of 2d August, 1786 — Shewing the Quotas assigned to each, the Amount / paid thereon, and the Balances due / ..... / Treasury of the United States / Register's Office [in MS. " 1 January 1787 Joseph Nourse, Register "].
Oblong f°. Broadside. S.D.

Apr. 13. **Letter to the States.**

437. United States in Congress assem- / bled, / April 13, 1787. / The following Letter was unanimously agreed to.
F°. pp. (3). S.D.

Prepared by John Jay.

Apr. 16. **Accounts.**

438. The Board of Treasury to whom was referred a motion for repealing the ordi- / nance of the 13th of October last, and that the Board be directed to report an ordi- / nance for the expeditious and equitable settlement of the accounts between the United / States and the Individual States, — Beg leave to report the following ordinance : — / Be it Ordained by the United States in Congress Assembled. / [signed] Samuel Osgood, / Walter Livingston. / April 16, 1787.
F°. Broadside. S.D.

Apr. 21. **Resolutions on Western Lands.**

439. By the United States in Congress / assembled, / April 21st, 1787.
F°. Broadside. V.S.

Apr. 26. Report on North West Territory.

440. The Committee, consisting of Mr. Johnson, Mr. Pinckney, Mr. Smith, Mr. Dane, and Mr. / Henry, appointed to prepare a Plan of a Temporary Government for / such Districts, or new States, as shall be laid out by the United States, upon the Principles of the Acts of Cession from individual States, and admitted into the Confederacy, — / F°. Broadside. **S.D.**

Apr. Report on Land Ordinance.

441. The Committee, consisting of Mr. Carrington, Mr. Varnum, Mr. Clarke, Mr. King and Mr. / Hawkins, to whom was referred a motion of Mr. Carrington for revising the ordinance for sur- / veying and selling the western territory, — report as follows : / .....
F°. Broadside. **S.D.**

June. Post Office Ordinance.

442. An Ordinance / for regulating the Post-Office of the United States of America.
F°. **S.D.**
Read the first time Feb. 14.

July 10. Report on Parsons.

443. The Committee consisting of [blank] to whom was / referred the Memorial of Samuel Holden Parsons, / Esquire, report as follows. / .....
F°. Broadside. **S.D.**

July 13. Ordinance of 1787.

444. An Ordinance for the Government of the Territo- / ry of the United States, North-West of the River / Ohio. F°. 1 l. **V.S., S.D.**

July 18. Treaty with Morocco.

445. The United States of America, in / Congress assembled. / To All who shall see these Presents, Greeting. F°. 2 ll. **V.S.**

July 20. Report on Indian Affairs.

446. The Secretary of the United States for the depart- / ment of War, to whom were referred certain Papers / transmitted by the Superintendant of Indian Af- / fairs for the Northern department. / Reports, / ..... [Signed] H. Knox / War Office, July 20, 1787. F°. 1 l. **S.D.**

Aug. 3. Report on Southern Indians.

447. The Committee consisting of Mr. Kearney, Mr. Car- / rington, Mr. Bingham, Mr. Smith and Mr. Dane, / to whom was referred the Report of the Secretary / at War, and Sundry Papers relative to Indian Affairs in / the Southern Department; and also a motion of the / Delegates from the State of Georgia, / Report, / ..... F°. 1 l. **S.D.**
See *Journals* for Oct. 10, 1786.

Sept. 25. Requisitions for 1787.

448. Schedule of Requisitions on the several States by the U. S. in Congress assembled; / ..... / [signed] Joseph Nourse.
Oblong f°. **V.S.**

Sept. 28. Report of Board of Treasury.

449. The Board of Treasury, to whom "it was / referred to report a Requisition for the current year, in- / cluding one year's Interest on the Foreign Debt, and such part / of the Principal as may become due in the ensuing year; and / providing for the Payment of one year's Interest on the Do- / mestic Debt, in a mode most con-venient to the States, and / advantageous to the Union." / Beg leave with great Deference to represent to Congress, / 4°. pp. 14. **V.S.**
See No. 453.

Sept. 28. Proposed Constitution.

450. We the People of the United States, in order to / form a more perfect Union, establish Justice, / insure domestic Tranquility, provide for the / common Defense, promote the general Wel- / fare, and secure the Blessings of Liberty to / ourselves and our Posterity, do ordain and / establish this Constitution for the United / States of America. F°. pp. 4. **S.D.**
This is the edition of the proposed Constitution, printed for the Continental Congress.

Sept. Report on Civil List.

451. The Committee, consisting of Mr. Dane, Mr. Clark, Mr. Varnum, Mr. Lee, and Mr. Grayson to / whom it was referred to consider what Officers / in the Civil Department are become unneces- / sary; and to whom also was referred a Motion of / Mr. Dane, respecting the Department of the / Treasury — report the following Resolutions. / ..... F°. Broadside. **S.D.**

Oct. 3. Resolutions on Frontier Troops.

452. By the United States in Con- / gress Assembled. / October 3. 1787.
F°. Broadside. **S.**

Oct. 11. Requisitions for 1787.

453. By the United States In Con- / gress assembled / October 11, 1787.
F°. 2 ll. **S., P.L.**
Report of the Committee on the Report of the Board of Treasury (No. 449).

Oct. 12. Report on Northern Indians.

454. The Committee, consisting of Mr. Dane, Mr. Hawkins, Mr. Kean, Mr. Irvine, and Mr. / Carrington, to whom were referred the Report of the Secretary at War, and sundry Pa- / pers relative to Indian Affairs in the Northern Department; — Report in Part : / F°. Broadside. **S.D.**

Instructions for Indian Superintendents.

455. Instructions to [MS. "the"] / Superintendant of Indian Affairs for the [ ] Department. / F°. Broadside. **P.L.**

Journals. 1786–7.

456. Journal / of the / United States / In Congress Assembled: / containing / The Proceedings / from / The Sixth Day of November, 1786, / to / The Fifth Day of November, 1787. / Vol. XII. / Published by Order of Congress. / M,DCC,LXXXVII. 8°. pp. 255, (9).

1788.

Jan. 1. Schedule of Requisitions.

457. Schedule / Of the Requisitions on the several States, by the United States in Congress assembled; / Of 10th Sept. 1782; 30th Oct. 1781, and 27th and 28th April, 1784; Of 27th Sept. 1785, 2d Aug. 1786; and of 11th Oct. 1787 : / Shewing the Quotas assigned to each, the Amount paid thereon, and the Balances due. [31 March 1788] / [signed] ..... Treasury of the United States, / Register's Office. [in MS. "Joseph Nourse / Register"].
Oblong f°. Broadside. **S.D.**
Endorsed, in ink, "1st January 1788. Joseph Nourse Register."

Mar. 19. Report on Land Ordinance.

458. A Supplement to an Ordinance entitled, " An / Ordinance for ascertaining the mode of Disposing of Lands in the Western Territory." / F°. 1 l. P.L.

See No. 463.

May. Report on Western Lands.

459. The Committee, consisting of Mr. Wadsworth, Mr. Irvine, and Mr. White. to whom was referred the / Petition of the French and American inhabitants of Post St. Vincent's and the Illinois, by their Agent, Mr. Tardiveau, / beg leave to report, That as there is much uncertainty about the possessions of the inhabitants of the Country upon the Wabash / and Missisippi [sic] rivers, and the quantity of land that they may be entitled respectively to hold and enjoy, by rights acquired / before they became subjects of the United States; in order to quiet their minds, to maintain them in their just rights, and / extend to them the liberality of the United States, they submit the following resolutions, vis. / ..... F°. Broadside. S.D.

June 11. Report on Invalids.

460. By the United States in Congress / assembled, / June 11, / 1788. / On the report of a Committee consisting of Mr. Dane, / Mr. Hamilton and Mr. Brown, ... / . . who were ordered to take into Consideration the Invalid Esta- / blishment: F°. Broadside. V.S.

June 20. Report on Morgan.

461. The Committee consisting of [blank] to whom was / referred the Memorial of George Morgan, and his associates, respecting a tract of land in the / Illinois country, on the Missisippi, [sic] beg leave to report, ... / F°. Broadside. S.D.

The committee was Williamson, Dane, Carrington, Kearney, and Wingate.

June 20. Resolutions on Morgan.

462. By the United States in Congress / assembled, / June 20 1788. / F°. Broadside. P.L.

The report (No. 461) as adopted by the Congress.

July 9. Land Ordinance.

463. By the United States in Congress / assembled / July 9, 1788. / A Supplement to an ordinance entitled " An Ordinance for as- / certaining the Mode of disposing of lands in the Western Territory." F°. Broadside. S.V.S.

A different draft from No. 458, reported July 2, by Dane, Clark, Baldwin, Williamson, and Edwards.

Aug. 20. Report on Requisitions for 1788.

464. By the United States in Congress assembled, / Wednesday, August 20, 1788. F°. 1 l. P.L., S.

Made by Clark, Dane, Williamson, Bingham, and Baldwin.

Sept. 1. Proclamation in re Cherokees.

465. By the United States in Congress / Assembled, / A Proclamation. / ..... / Done in Congress, this First Day of September, in the Year of our Lord One / Thousand Seven Hundred and Eighty-eight ... / Cyrus Griffin, President. F°. Broadside. V.S.

Sept. 13. Resolutions in re New Governments.

466. By the United States in Congress / assembled, / September 13, 1788. F°. Broadside. V.S., S.

Appointing a day for the new government to assemble.

Consular Convention.

467. 1784.	1788.
Convention between His most | Christian Majesty and the thirteen | United States of North America, for | the purpose of determining and fix- | ing the functions and privileges of | their respective Consuls, vice-Con- | suls, Agents and Commissaries |	Convention between His Most | Christian Majesty and the United | States of America, for the purpose | of defining and establishing the | functions and prive leges of their res | pective Consuls and vice-Consuls. |

4°. pp. 10. S.D.

Journals. 1787-9.

468. Journal / of the / United States / in Congress Assembled : / Containing the / Proceedings / from / The 5th Day of November, 1787. / To / The 3d Day of November 1788. / Volume XIII. / Published by Order of Congress. / Printed by John Dunlap.

8°. pp. 170, xcviii (1), xi.

The Index is misprinted Vol. XIV.

Collected Works.

Collected Journals. Contemporary Edition.

These volumes were printed from time to time as already (No. 79) stated, and under the number following the collation given below will be found a title and note on each. In 1786 four of the volumes were reprinted by order of Congress, and these reprints are included in this series, as they are the volumes usually found with the bound sets. This collation is made from a comparison of three sets, but differs in several particulars from those given in Sabin, No. 15545.

Vol. I.	1774-5.	Aitken.	pp. (2), 310, (12).	No. 79.
Vol. II.	1776.	Dunlap.	pp. (2), 540, xxvii.	No. 125.
Vol. III.	1777.	Dunlap.	pp. 603, xxii.	No. 164.
Vol. III.	1777.	Patterson.	pp. 603, xxii.	
Vol. IV.	1778.	Claypoole.	pp. (2), 748, lxxxix, (4).	No. 158
Vol. V.	1779.	Claypoole.	pp. 464, (15), lxxiv.	No. 274.
Vol. VI.	1780.	Claypoole.	pp. 403, xxxviii, (3).	No. 295.
Vol. VI.	1780.	Dunlap.	pp. 257, xliii.	No. 296.
Vol. VII.	1781-2.	Claypoole.	pp. 522, (4), lxxix.	No. 321.
Vol. VII.	1781-2.	Patterson.	pp. 522, (17), lxxix.	No. 322.
Vol. VIII.	1782-3.	Claypoole.	pp. 483.	No. 345.
Vol. IX.	1783-4.	Dunlap.	pp. 317, xviii, 47.	No. 364.
Vol. X.	1784-5.	Dunlap.	pp. 368.	No. 402.
Vol. XI.	1785-6.	Dunlap.	pp. 267, xvi.	No. 435.
Vol. XII.	1786-7.	No printer.	pp. 255, (9).	No. 456.
Vol. XIII.	1787-9.	Dunlap.	pp. 170, xcviii, (1), xi.	No. 468.

Collected Journals. Edition of 1800.

470. Journals / of / Congress : / Containing their / Proceedings / from September 5, 1774, to January 1. 1776. / Published by Authority. / Vol. I. / From Folwell's Press. / Philadelphia. / 1800. 13 vols. 8°.

Vol. I. pp. (2), 289, (12).
Vol. II. pp. (2), 480, (22).
Vol. III. pp. (2), 488, (16).
Vol. IV. pp. 537, (42).
Vol. V. pp. (2), 349, (34).
Vol. VI. pp. (2), 176, (32).
Vol. VII. pp. 306, (18).
Vol. VIII. pp. 337, (14).
Vol. IX. pp. 227, (10), 29.
Vol. X. pp. 256, (14).
Vol. XI. pp. 193, (10).
Vol. XII. pp. 169, (5).
Vol. XIII. pp. 192, (2), (5).

Collected Journals. Edition of 1823.

471. Journals / of / The American Congress : / From 1774 to 1788. / In Four Volumes. / Volume I : / From September 5, 1774, to December

31, 1776, inclusive. / Washington : / Printed and
Published by Way and Gideon. / 1823.

4 vols. 8°.

Vol. I.   pp. (2), 588, xxviii.
Vol. II. pp. (2), 639, xxxviii.
Vol. III. pp. (2), 740, lviii.
Vol. IV. pp. (2), 880, 62, (2), lxvii.

Secret Journals.

472.   Secret Journals / of / The Acts and Proceedings / of / Congress, / from the first meeting thereof to the dissolution / of the Confederation, by the adoption / of the Constitution of
the / United States. / Published under the direction of the President of the United States,
conformably to / Resolution of Congress of
March 27, 1818, and April 21, 1820. / Vol. I. /
Boston : / Printed and Published by Thomas B.
Wait. / 1820.

4 vols. 8°.

Vol. I.   pp. 466.
Vol. II. pp. 587.
Vol. III. pp. 614.
Vol. IV. pp. 448.

31

THE END.

www.ingramcontent.com/pod-product-compliance
Lightning Source LLC
Chambersburg PA
CBHW061240260626
47172CB00003B/940